Patrick and Katherine's Second Chance

ALEX AND CHASTITY

BOOK FOUR

LEXIE MIERS

CHAPTER 1

Patrick

Walking in on my daughter, naked, in the arms of my best friend was not something I'd ever imagined happening to me. Not even in my worst nightmares.

Had I thought I'd one day accidentally catch Axel fucking some woman in his apartment or on his desk at work? *Sure.* He was a player, and a rich one at that. He had a different woman in his bed every other night.

But my daughter...? Never!

I used my key and walked into Axel's apartment a few days after Christmas day, expecting to find my best friend hard at work like he always was—the eternal workaholic. His parents were cold as ice and lived on the other side of the world, so he wouldn't be busy with family stuff, that was for sure.

To be honest, I'd been worried about him. He'd sounded like absolute shit when I last spoke to him the day after Christmas, and I wanted to make sure he was doing okay.

I froze when I saw Axel naked and kissing a girl perched on the edge of the marble countertop in his kitchen. My first instinct was to turn around and walk away. No one wanted to be *that guy* who ruined a mate's hookup. But then I'd heard the young woman's familiar giggle, and her blonde hair caught my eye as being disturbingly similar to my daughter's.

Oh, hell no! Rage instantly consumed me. "Chastity!" I roared. "What the hell are you doing here?"

She gasped and covered her chest with her arms, her face stricken. "Dad!"

Axel turned his back to cover my daughter. "Pat, go wait in the living room."

I gaped at him. "Axel. What the fuck?" He was ordering me about like I was some subordinate who worked for him? *Fuck that for a joke!*

"Just go," he commanded again. "We'll be there in a minute."

Steam and fury poured through me, but the very last thing I wanted to see was the two of them, naked, doing the walk of shame back to the bedroom to re-dress. *Gross.* I stomped off to the living room so I couldn't see them any longer. I could hear their footsteps on the floors, then a door shut.

I sat on the couch and buried my face in my hands, equal parts enraged and physically ill. How long had this been going on? Had they met at my birthday party? Was this the girl Axel had been telling me about? *Oh God. Oh... shit!*

I ran my hands through my hair and lifted my head, inhaling deeply and praying for divine intervention. Surely, I was dreaming, right? I wasn't actually sitting in my best friend's living room, waiting for my daughter and best friend to return and explain why they were about to have sex in his kitchen. It just... couldn't be my reality. It couldn't!

A minute or more later, they walked back into the room. Dressed once more, thank the heavens.

I stayed sitting in the armchair and watched them approach, my disgust barely contained. I felt like a grenade with the pin pulled, ready to explode.

Chastity was pale and drawn, her lower lip trembling like she was going to cry.

I steeled myself against the soft emotions within me that always gave in to her when she pouted like that.

Chastity sat on the sofa to my right, hand twisted in her lap.

Axel stood over near the sofa on my left.

Bastard. "So," I managed to say, taking a deep breath and trying to remain calm. "How long has this been going on? Since my birthday?" If they met there and started dating immediately after, that would be the biggest insult. I hadn't seen them talking all that much that night, but that didn't mean anything, necessarily.

"No!" Chastity quickly denied. "We met at the gym, and we had no idea who each other was. We went on a few dates and *then* found out that you two knew each other."

I sat up straighter and slid to the edge of the chair. "And when you found out Axel was my best friend, what did you do, Chastity?" Surely that must have come as a shock to them?

"We, ah..." She stared at me with tears in her eyes. "We broke up."

Bullshit! I jumped to my feet, anger exploding inside my gut with scarcely restrained fire. "Then what the fuck is going on here?" I yelled.

Chastity sobbed, then covered her mouth with her hand, obviously overcome in the moment and unsure of how to proceed.

Axel, the traitor, got to his feet slowly. "Pat, look. I'm sorry you found out this way. It's not ideal in any way."

I stared at Axel, stupefied. I thought he was smarter than that. He was a billionaire businessman for fuck's sake! He must have a brain cell between his two ears! "Not ideal?" I repeated. "You were up here *fucking* my daughter, Axel."

Axel put his hands up in surrender. "I'm sorry, Pat."

"You're not sorry," I ground out, sinking back onto the lounge. *Fucking liar.*

Axel opened his mouth to speak again.

I put up my hand to stop him from apologizing again. "And don't even start! You have no idea how I feel, Axel. *No* idea!"

"No, I don't," Axel agreed, his tone calm.

Too calm for my liking. I was fucking furious over here and he was... what? Relaxed about the fact our friendship was over? Just chill about the worst situation I'd encountered in my life? "No, you don't. Because you don't have any kids," I hissed at him. "And why don't you?"

"I'm sure you're going to tell me," Axel muttered, staring down at the carpet at his feet.

I ignored his childish behavior and yelled the truth in his face. "Because you're a selfish, narcissistic asshole!"

"Dad!" Chastity protested, jumping to her feet. "You can't talk to him like that."

I whirled on my daughter, my only child. "I've known Axel since you were in elementary school, sweetheart. You don't get to tell me how I speak to him."

Tears filled her eyes again. "But Dad—"

"No!" I growled at her. "I'm disgusted with you. Disgusted with you both." Then I turned on Axel. "You're twenty years older than her, for fuck's sake!" Why did neither of them realize this was a problem? A *massive* problem.

"We know that," Axel explained softly. "This was only meant to be a holiday fling. Nothing serious."

Did he just say that? Did he seriously just fucking say that to my damn face? I marched up to him and shoved Axel in the chest with both hands. "You bastard. You take my daughter... *my daughter*, and convince her to have some slutty affair? She's better than that, Axel, and you know it!"

"It wasn't his fault, Dad," Chastity said. "I was the one who begged him to date me for the couple of weeks I was here. He didn't want to go on after we found out the connection, but I—"

I flicked my hand to dismiss her. "You're a child, Chastity. You don't know anything about this guy."

"Excuse me?" Chastity said, her cheeks flushed red.

I ignored her, my anger directed at my former best friend. I pointed my finger at Axel. "You and I are done, you got it? Come on, Chastity. We're going home."

"Dad, please stop. I know this is a shock, but I'm almost twenty-two. And I like Axel. He's been great for me!"

I turned toward my daughter, amazed by the words coming out of her mouth. *How could she be so naïve?* So stupid. "You have no idea how I'm feeling, Chastity. Shock doesn't even come close to covering it. And as for Axel, I fail to see how some rich player who's slept with half the women in the city can be *good* for you. You've got your whole life ahead of you!"

"Dad, stop!" Chastity gasped. "You have no idea about our relationship, or how amazing Axel has been to me."

Amazing? Give me a break. "Yeah," I rolled my eyes. "I'm sure he turned on the charm to get in your pants, Chastity. But don't expect him to stick around. He created the saying, '*hit it and quit it*'."

"Stop!" Chastity yelled back, anger flashing in her eyes.

I flinched.

"I love him, Dad. I love him! He's amazing. And even if this fling lasts only two weeks, I'm happy. How can you not see that?"

I stared at my daughter, my young, beautiful and apparently, very naïve daughter. *Is she serious?*

"What?" Chastity repeated, flicking her hair indignantly like a model in a commercial.

I swallowed hard, my nightmare continuing. "Did you just say you *love* him?"

"Uh..." Chastity faltered. "Yeah... I..."

That bastard! I turned on Axel. I'd known he liked to play around, but he'd always shown respect to the women he slept with at least. He made sure they knew what they were signing up for and didn't get hurt. But this...? I hadn't thought he was capable of this. It was a new low for the man I'd considered my best friend. I threw my hands up in the air. "Now she loves you? Fucking hell, man! Why'd you have to go and screw with my daughter, of all people?"

Axel turned on my daughter, his expression stoic. "That wasn't the deal, Chastity."

I shoved Axel again. "What did you just say? She says she loves you and you say that wasn't the deal?" Surely, Axel must have known that by sleeping with an innocent, her feelings were going to become involved? He wasn't that fucking daft, was he?

For the first time, Axel glared at me. "It wasn't! I told her what was on offer, and she said she was happy with it."

I swung before I made the conscious decision to hit him. Hard and fast, my fist shot out in rage, at the injustice of the vile words spilling from his lips. *Cr-aaack!* Impact. Pain exploded up my wrist. "You're a smug bastard," I accused with venom. I grabbed Chastity's arm. "Let's go."

"Axel..." she whispered.

Axel wiped at the blood dripping from his lip. "Go."

"But—" she began.

"Chastity. Go. There's nothing more to say."

I looked away. The off-beat love scene was making me sick.

"Wait! Let me grab my bag," Chastity said, pulling away.

"Where is it?" I asked, curious about their set-up.

"The bedroom," she answered.

I laughed. "How was it sleeping in that bed by yourself all night? Bit lonely?" It was a cruel thing to say, but I wasn't feeling particularly charitable at the moment.

She turned and frowned at me. "What do you mean?"

I crossed my arms over my chest. "Everyone knows Axel won't sleep with his women. He spends more time in the guest room than his own bedroom." Something I'd always considered a genius move, from a male perspective. A bastard move.

Chastity stared straight at me. "Well, that shows just how much you don't know him, Dad. Axel's slept with me, all night, every night we've been together."

My mouth dropped open. *He... what? No. That meant— Oh, no.* I turned on my best friend, who was still wiping his bleeding mouth. "Is she telling the truth, Axel?"

He lifted his head, locking gazes with me. "Yeah," he returned. "So what?"

"So what?" I repeated, surprised once more about how stupid this guy really was capable of being. "So that means—" I took a breath. "Oh my God. You love her too!" I would have slammed my head into a wall if there was one close enough, and for the second time in a matter of minutes, I wanted to punch Axel in his damn face.

Chastity walked back into the room with a bag in hand.

"You ready?" I asked her, though I was still reeling from what I'd just learned. That meant Axel hadn't been just playing with Chastity, he was in love with her.

And she thought she was in love with him, which meant this whole scenario was even more fucked up than I first thought.

"Uh, yeah."

We walked into the elevator and went down to the parking garage.

My head was whirling with impossible words and feelings, and all of it was too much to deal with.

Chastity and I didn't speak the whole time. We walked to the car in silence and drove to her mom's house.

Her eyes were shiny like she was trying not to cry, but a tear trailed down her cheek as she opened the front door.

I walked up behind her, something I hadn't done since she was in pre-school. I opened my mouth to speak to her, but she was gone before I'd gotten my thoughts in order.

She left the door hanging open, and that's when my ex-wife walked out, confusion written all over her tired face. "Patrick? What's wrong? What are you doing here?"

I groaned, a little part of me dying inside. Now, this was going to take some telling.

CHAPTER 2

Katherine/Kaiti

It had been so long since I'd seen Patrick. *So long.* I'd almost forgotten how good looking he was. Annoyingly so, was the answer. He had dark hair that curled around his ear, a soft dimple in his right cheek, and his arms... *Damn.* He'd gotten buff, no longer the lanky young man I'd married decades ago.

"Uh, it's a long story," Patrick said, in answer to my question. "We — um, I need to tell you... I need to talk to you."

I could literally feel my eyebrows lift so high on my forehead they almost reached my hairline. "Ah—" *Here? Now? Why now?*

Patrick had never been inside my house, but we'd managed to co-parent our daughter with a relative degree of success. Emails, texts, a few phone calls here and there. But we'd never sat down and talked face to face like friends. Though something told me whatever he needed to say now was more important than anything we'd ever had to deal with before.

I weighed up what I knew so far, talking out aloud. "Well, considering Chastity was at Axel's place, and you just brought her home in tears..." This was serious. "Do you want come in?"

It was time for Patrick's eyebrows to climb his forehead. "Ah, yeah. I could use a drink, actually."

Mr. Health Freak having a drink on a Monday morning? "Hm. Okay. Come in."

We walked down the short hallway and into the kitchen.

I waved around at the relatively clean house I kept. "Excuse the mess." There were still Christmas presents hanging around, and my tree was still up.

"It's... nice, Kaiti," he said, glancing around and taking it all in.

The nickname rolled over me like a warm shower, then jolted me back to reality just as fast. It had been too long since I'd heard him call me that. He was the only one who'd ever used that nickname.

That was when I noticed what he was wearing. A black tank that showed off his ripped arms and well-defined chest, a pair of sneakers and gray track pants. "You look like you're going for a run..." I observed. "What happened?" I went to the fridge and stared at the bottle of white wine in the rack on the door. I didn't carry beer or anything more typically masculine. "Your choices are Moscato, coffee, or herbal tea."

"No whiskey?" he asked, running his hand through his thick, dark hair.

"That bad?" I asked.

He nodded.

"Well, I don't have any hard liquor, I'm sorry."

"Just coffee, then, please. Black."

"One sugar?" I prompted.

He stared at me for a long moment before responding. "Yeah."

I turned away, annoyed I'd slipped up that easily. I still remembered every detail about my ex-husband. From the way he took his coffee, to the way he liked his cock sucked. Hard, and with just a little bit of teeth. I shook myself. *Get it together!* I chastised myself. This was one of the many reasons I couldn't be around Patrick. I didn't feel like myself. I felt weak, like I was young and impressionable all over again.

I flicked on the coffee machine and whirled around. He'd knocked me off guard coming over like this, but I needed to remember he was an ex-husband for a reason. *A very good reason.* He'd left me and moved on with one of my college friends in less than a minute; leaving me with a two-year-old, and—nothing. Nowhere to live, no way to support myself. I'd been royally fucking screwed.

I crossed my arms over my chest, stoking the fire inside my belly. "Okay, tell me. Spit it out, Patrick. Why is our daughter in her bedroom crying like her heart is broken?"

Patrick sighed, pulled out a stool and sat down at the kitchen counter. "Probably because it is. I think they just broke up."

And that was all it took to have the walls around my heart come crumbling down again. I glanced at the hallway that led to her bedroom. "I should go speak to her," I said, the mother in me flaring to life. I hadn't always been the best mom, but I never wanted Chastity to hurt.

"Uh, I need to tell you something first."

I narrowed my gaze at him. There were red slashes over his cheekbones that spoke of anger or embarrassment. "Okay. Give me a second then." I made his coffee as well as one for myself, then pushed his mug across the counter, staying on my side on purpose. The more physical space between Patrick and me, the better.

"Go."

He took a fortifying sip of the coffee then looked me right in the eye, the intensity rolling right down to my socks. "I just walked in on them... together."

I pressed my free hand against the cold countertop to steady myself. "As in... together-together?" *As in, having sex?* My stomach rolled at the very idea of it.

"Well, they weren't, you know, into it yet. But they were naked, and well, let's just say I'm glad I wasn't a few minutes later."

I put my hand over my mouth, stupefied. I actually felt sorry for my ex-husband now. What a horrible thing for a father to witness! Then logic clicked into place, and I had questions galore. "Hang on a second. Chastity was at Axel's apartment... How could you have walked in on them?"

Now Patrick looked downright miserable.

"Because Axel is my best friend, Kaiti."

What? "Sorry? Come again?" I asked.

He groaned as though frustrated. "Axel is my best friend! As in, someone I have known for over ten years. I have a key to his apartment and he has a key to mine. We train together every week. *He's my best friend,*" he said, stressing the words.

Saying it twice like that made everything so much worse. "I... I don't know what to say." I was shocked. Then it hit me. *Oh my God.* I knew I'd seen his face somewhere before, but I couldn't think of where! I must have seen Axel with Patrick, in a photo or in real life at some point... *Fuck!*

"Me, either!" Patrick confided, then slumped. "He is such a player. But he's usually an honest one. He doesn't fool around with young girls like Chastity. He dates models and women who want him for his money. He knows what they want, they know what he wants, it's mutual."

I crossed my arms over my chest and leaned on the counter. "Then what the hell is he doing with our daughter?" Because my daughter was not a gold-digger, and she sure as hell wasn't experienced enough to be chasing older players; that just wasn't her.

Patrick ran his hand through his hair and blew out an exasperated breath. "I don't know. They said they met by chance, and just... Oh, for fucks' sake, Kaiti! She said she loves him."

"She does," I agreed with him. "As much as she can at twenty-two. It's her first love."

Patrick pinned me with a stare that I felt to my bones. By twenty-two, we were already married, and I'd had Chastity.

"You know what I mean," I said, glancing away.

"I do, which is why I dismissed Chastity's feelings initially, but..."

"But what?"

Patrick looked down, running his finger along a flaw in the wooden countertop. "I think he loves her too."

My jaw dropped open. "They've known each other for barely a month!"

Patrick's gaze flew up to mine again. "I didn't know that, but it doesn't change anything. I *know* Axel, and he cares about her a hell of a lot more than he's letting on."

"I doubt that," I muttered. Guys like him didn't feel anything, especially deep love. They were as shallow as my damn frying pan.

Patrick didn't correct me but judging by the look in his eyes, he was still thinking about it.

The silence stretched between us, and although part of me wanted to make small talk and extend this strange little chat, I desperately wanted to go talk to our daughter. "I better go see how Chastity is," I said, taking a few steps toward the front door. "Is there anything else I should know?" *Other than the fact that they broke up, Axel was Patrick's best friend, and the feelings they had for each other were uncertain?*

Patrick stood up from his stool and followed me to the front door. "Not really, Kaiti, but—"

"Don't worry about Chastity," I assured him. "I'll sort her out."

He nodded, his eyes becoming shadowed and dark. "I know you will. You've done a great job with her, Kaiti. She's a beautiful young woman."

I could tell it hurt him to say it. But whether it was because it was a compliment to me, or because he'd just been confronted with her naked, I wasn't sure. Regardless, I just pasted on a fake smile. "Thanks for bringing her home." I began to shut the front door.

Patrick thrust out an arm, blocking me. "Can you let me know what happens?"

"Uh... you mean..."

"Call me? Or text." He shrugged. "Whatever suits you best."

I inhaled sharply, a strange feeling swirling around my insides. "Sure. I'll let you know what she says."

"Okay. And I'll let you know if I find out anything else. Same number?"

I nodded. "Yep."

Patrick smiled, waved, and walked away.

And like an idiot, I just watched him go. *Damn he has a fine ass.* I slammed the door shut before my hormones could make me feel any more crazy things I didn't want to feel anymore.

Locking the door, I turned toward the bedrooms. My house was small, with only two bedrooms and one living space, but it was mine. Mercifully, my parents had given me the money for the down payment after Patrick and I had divorced. Then I'd managed to pay it off by working nights and weekends while Chastity was little, before finishing my teaching degree when she was older.

I blew out my breath and walked to Chastity's room. Despite her being at college for almost four years now, the pink letters of her name still decorated the bedroom door. I hadn't changed a thing while she'd been gone. I lifted my hand and knocked out of courtesy.

"Come in."

The door squeaked as I opened it, then seeing my daughter curled up on her bed, her eyes red from crying, I couldn't stay away from her any longer. I walked straight across the room and sat down, the mattress dipping, thanks to my fat ass. "Your dad told me what happened. I'm so sorry, Chastity."

She stared up at me. "You and Dad actually talked?"

I almost laughed but didn't. "Yeah. I even made him coffee and he sat at the breakfast bar." Something he'd never done before.

Chastity pulled herself up to lean against the headboard, still sniffling. "No way."

This time I laughed. "Yeah, well, what can I say? It's a Christmas miracle."

Chastity's gaze dropped and her eyes filled with tears. "More like you two finally had a reason to talk about your troublesome, delinquent daughter. I've never really given you a reason to get together before, have I?"

My heart broke for my daughter. *My good girl.* "No, you haven't."

Silence filled the room as Chastity wiped the tears from her flushed face.

I needed to say something, but where to start? "Chastity, I'm so sorry. I knew I recognized Axel from somewhere but couldn't work out the *where.* It must have been when I'd been around your father's place at some point."

"Or on his Facebook profile?" she teased, knowing I checked up on him from time to time.

I felt my cheeks flush with heat. *Probably.* "I'm still sorry I didn't realize sooner." Maybe that would have saved her all this heartbreak.

Chastity stared down at her lap. "We broke up when we first found out about the connection to Dad, but we couldn't stay away from each other. We didn't want to. So, it's my fault as much as Axel's. We knew what we were doing, but we just hoped—"

"You'd get away with it?" I finished for her with a heavy sigh. The things the young tell themselves... I remembered it all too well. "So, what was the plan? Just have a Christmas fling, then forget about him?" It was a horrible plan for a girl with a heart as big and soft as Chastity's, but I could imagine her trying to be like everyone else.

She'd gone to spring break a few years ago and tried to be like everyone else then too; dancing and drinking the nights away until she had ended up calling me to come get her. She *wasn't* like anyone else, and I'd thought she realized that already. She was special.

Chastity nodded. "Yeah, I thought I could."

I shook my head. "I knew you wouldn't."

"What do you mean?"

I pushed my hair back off my face, willing myself to be gentle as I told my daughter the truth. "Oh, honey, you've been head over heels in love with him since your first date. Axel isn't the sort of guy you just see a few times then get over."

He was the stuff dreams and romance novels were made from. For me, that meant he was dangerous with a capital D. For someone like Chasity, she would have only seen the positive, more dreamy qualities.

"What sort of guy is he?"

I tilted my head and said softly. "The sort that breaks your heart. Then you have to spend the next ten years trying to get over him, desperately picking up the pieces."

"Was that who Dad was for you, too?" she asked.

I froze like a deer in headlights. *Am I that transparent?* "Yeah, he was," I admitted heavily.

"And now?" she asked. "What is he, now?"

I shrugged because there was no good or easy answer to that question. Part of me would always love Patrick. He'd been my first love, my only husband, and the father of my child.

"It's too late for him to be anything to me now, Chastity. I made some mistakes, and so did he. And in the end, we didn't find our way back to each other. Even though, over the years, I'd kind of hoped we would."

I glanced away, not quite believing that I'd just admitted that to my daughter out aloud. That was something I only whispered to myself in privacy and regret, inside my own head. Then I'd skitter away from the thought as if it had burned me just as quickly.

Chastity squeezed my hand, her heart in her eyes. "I'm sorry, Mom."

Oh, my beautiful girl. Only she could find such empathy in her soul, even after her own heart was broken. I squeezed her hand back. "And I'm sorry for you, sweetheart. I wish I could have saved you the heartache."

Chastity took a deep breath and sighed. She was looking brighter now, her eyes no longer filled with tears. "I don't regret it," she said. "Being with Axel was the happiest I've ever been, I think."

Well, that was good to know. Hopefully in years to come she'd look back on her first love with fondness, even if that felt impossible now. But I had to ask. "And what happened with your dad?"

"Yeah, I could have done without that part," she said, grimacing.

I could only imagine how horrifying that would have been for her. It had been bad enough that I'd had to tell my parents that I was pregnant at twenty-one and dropping out of college. But I'd never had my parents walk in on me having sex. *Thank God.* "I bet you could have." I got to my feet and started backing toward the door. "How about I make us some pasta for lunch, put on a movie, and we can veg out on the couch?" I offered, hoping some girl time would help her bounce back.

"Thanks, Mom. I'll be there in a minute."

I left her room and went straight to the kitchen. Patrick's coffee cup sat on the counter, still warm. I picked it up to wash it but held it in my hand a minute longer than I should have, just feeling the memory of the imprint of his palm against mine.

CHAPTER 3

Patrick

I'd scheduled the week off between Christmas and New Year's so that I could spend more time with Chastity. After all, she was home so infrequently now that she was in college. But after what happened a few days ago between us, I didn't know what to do with myself or how to approach her. Not to mention I'd just broken up with the woman I'd been seeing, and Axel and I were on the outs, obviously, so I felt at a complete loss. I seriously had no idea what to do with my time.

So, when the phone rang, I jumped for it. It was a friend of mine from the health club. "Hey, Carl. How're you doing? Merry Christmas."

"Hey, man. Good. Good. How are you doing?"

I glanced around my spotless apartment. "Ah, yeah, I'm good, too. Kind of bored with all the time off though."

"You? Bored?" he scoffed. "That's a first. Where's the redhead you've been dating?"

Who? "Redhead… Oh, that was a few months ago. Carrie was blonde."

Carl laughed uproariously. "Man, seriously? Between you and Axel, I think you've got most of the city covered."

I ground my teeth together, hating being thrown into the same basket as that guy, but I didn't want to take it out on Carl, so I just half-heartedly agreed. "Yeah, maybe."

"So, what happened this time?"

I huffed out a bitter laugh. "She tried to tell me she was on the pill, but she wasn't." Too many women had tried that trick on me. Too many to count. They thought that once they were pregnant, I'd marry them, or at least stick around. They couldn't have chosen a worse guy to try that on. I'd made that mistake once. Never again. I guarded my sperm with my life.

"Whoa. You have the worst luck. But you know those women are few and far between."

I rolled my eyes. "Spoken by a guy whose been married for twenty years to the same woman."

Carl thought women were angels, and I had to admit that his wife was one of the good ones. "Yeah... well..."

"Hey, you have time to catch up for a drink later?" I asked, suddenly desperate to get out of the apartment.

"Yeah, sure. You want to come here?" Carl asked.

And watch him and his missus fawn all over their four kids? *No, thank you.* "How about you come here?" I countered. "The game's on."

"Let me check with Milly and I'll text you later."

That was a no, then. I struggled to keep my tone neutral, but I think I managed it. "Okay, cool. See you, man." I hung up, disappointed. This was usually when I'd call Axel and catch up with him. Axel worked like a maniac and partied like one, too. And since he barely slept, he managed to get all his work done and found the time to drink, chew the fat, or party.

I growled aloud and began pacing my apartment. This was shit. I liked being a bachelor. Not answering to anyone, except in moments like these. It was fucking lonely. My phone buzzed and I frowned. Who was messaging now? My stomach tightened when I read the sender's name. *The Ex.*

Hey, Patrick. I just wanted to let you know that Chastity went back to school this morning. I told her to drop in and say

goodbye, but I don't think she did. Just thought you should know.

I flopped down onto the couch and ran a hand through my hair, squeezing my skull for emphasis. "Shit." I typed right back.

She didn't come by, so thanks for letting me know.

I hit send, then stared at the message. Seeing her the other day had actually been nice. Better than expected. *I wonder if she's seeing anyone at the moment?* There was every chance that she could be just as lonely as me. After all, she was on Christmas break, and Chastity had gone back to college a week early. I began typing again.

You want to catch up for another coffee and talk about Chastity? Neutral ground this time. I'd like to hear what happened after I left.

I sent it before I changed my mind, a weird mix of anxiety and excitement fueled swirls occurring simultaneously in my gut.

There are a few things to tell you, actually. How about Rusty's?

I grinned. Rusty's was a cafe perfectly situated between our two homes.

Sure. I'm free now. You?

I waited, my shoulders tight with tension. Shit, maybe I'd pushed it too far. We hadn't communicated so openly this way in forever.

Yeah. I can meet you there in forty-five minutes. That suit?

More relieved than I'd like to admit, I tapped out my response.

See you then.

Needing a quick shower, I jumped to my feet. By the time the forty-five minutes had elapsed, I was already at Rusty's, standing outside, feeling stupidly nervous. *Should I go in and grab a table?* I wondered. No, that felt too much like a date move; and this was just two parents catching up to talk about their wayward daughter. Which was something I'd never had to do with Kaiti before. Ever.

"Hey," she said as she approached, wearing black leggings and a long purple sweater with a black belt tucking her waist in. She looked stunning, as usual.

"Hey," I greeted her back. "Do you want to grab a table inside... or?"

"Yeah, inside, please," she said, and forged ahead into the cafe, grabbing a booth in the back.

I followed, because that's what you did with Kaiti. You followed or you were left behind.

"Can we order a coffee first?" she asked suddenly, taking off her oversized sunglasses so I could see her lovely face.

"Of course."

The waitress came by, and we ordered, then the girl swept away again.

It was awkward for a moment, so I dove straight in. If we were talking about Chastity, we'd be fine. I was so sure of it. "So? What happened the other day after I left? You said you were going to tell me."

Kaiti nodded and sighed, resting her arms on the table. "She was so much more mixed up than I'd anticipated."

"What do you mean?" I pressed.

"I knew she had fallen head over heels for him—after all, she's young. This is her first love. And he made her feel special and wanted," she explained.

I nodded, anger gripping my gut instantly. "So, he fooled her into thinking she loved him? What an asshole." I'd always known it but had never seen it first-hand. The way Axel told his stories, he always chose women who wanted a good time and no permanent attachments. It was just fun for everyone.

Personally, I hadn't found a lot of those, myself. But Axel had managed to stay single forever, and had never been caught up in a major scandal, a fake pregnancy, or suffered any messy entanglements. I'd thought that'd meant something. Until now.

Katherine stared down into her coffee, a grimace tweaking the corners of her lips. "No," she said almost regretfully. "She loves him."

I frowned at her. "What's the problem, Kaiti? I know Chastity's upset and all, but she'll get over it, right? She's young, and they've broken up."

"But she doesn't have any closure," Kaiti said. "They just had a fight, and she was forced to leave. She still wants him—she's just mad at him."

Still not understanding the problem, I kept my mouth shut, drank my coffee, and waited for her to continue. *Maybe I'll never completely understand women*, I mused to myself.

And eventually, she did. "I mean... I hate that she was sucked in by a guy like that. I thought I'd taught her better."

I smiled. "You got her to twenty-two, practically innocent, Kaiti. I'd say that's the definition of a success story."

Kaiti looked up at me. "She was an innocent, Patrick. Axel was her first."

I groaned and glanced away. *God damn it.* "Not something I wanted to know." And just another reason I had to want to kill him. *At least he would have known what he was doing, unlike my first time with Kaiti.* "Anyway..." I rushed in, pushing those thoughts from my mind. "So, what you're telling me is, our daughter is heartbroken about the break-up, but she'd take Axel back if he begged her?"

It was Kaiti's turn to shudder. "I suppose so. But a guy like that... He wouldn't beg. Would he?"

I laughed at that. "Uh... no. No way."

Axel wasn't the sort of guy to throw himself on his own sword. It just wouldn't happen. Not for Chastity, not for anyone.

I drank my coffee and enjoyed the quiet around us. It was one of the things I'd always liked about Kaiti. I was content when I was around her. I never had to worry about filling the silence, usually because she was already filling it.

"Okay," she said, nodding to herself as if the matter were resolved. "So, we don't have anything to worry about, then. Chastity will finish college, go to chiropractic school, and will have the life we never got to have."

The old saying hit me right in the chest, hard and unexpected. "Hey, we did okay, Kaiti. Don't say it like that."

"Oh, I never regretted having Chastity. She's the best thing I ever did," Kaiti admitted, running her red-painted fingernail around the lip of her coffee cup. "But there was a lot we planned to do that we never got to, Patrick. Or I never did."

"You bought yourself a house," I reminded her, one of the many items on the to-do list that I'd never gotten around to.

"Yeah, but it has no yard and is practically falling down. Maybe when I retire, I'll knock it down and build my dream home."

It was on the very tip of my tongue to ask her what sort of house her dream home might be, but I knew that was one rabbit hole I didn't want to go down. "You've travelled," I added.

She cocked an eyebrow at me. "One trip to Hawaii does *not* count."

I nodded and stayed quiet. When we'd been in school, we'd had plans to travel together, and work. Then we'd wanted to marry and settle down later, after we'd done everything, we'd ever wanted to do. But when Kaiti had fallen pregnant, well... we'd done exactly what our parents had urged us to do. We'd married, dropped out of college, and forever lost our chance at the dream.

"Are you seeing anyone at the moment?" Kaiti asked suddenly.

I laughed. "Where did that come from?" We'd never asked each other about our love lives since splitting, or at least, not anymore. In the first few years after our separation, she'd shot her fair share of barbs at me about my dating life.

She shrugged. "Chastity just made a comment the other day that kind of stuck with me."

"What comment was that?" I asked, curious.

Kaiti grinned suddenly. "I told her that people would think she has Daddy issues, and she said she didn't. She argued that she had a great father who was always there for her. One who'd never remarried and bever had more kids to detract from her." She looked down.

"Well, neither did you," I reminded her, my heart aching from just looking at her.

Kaiti glanced back up and stared straight at me. "That's exactly what I told her." Then she chewed on her lip in that nervous way that I'd always loved. It made me want to kiss her, and the very thought of it had me grabbing for the menu to distract myself. "Could we order some lunch? I'm kind of hungry, now. The food here smells good."

"Uh, yeah... sure."

We called the waitress over and ordered some sandwiches but soon enough, the conversation turned back to dating.

"You didn't answer my question before," she reminded me.

She really wants to know? "No. I'm not seeing anyone. Are you?"

She shook her head. "Oh, God, no. I'm way too old for that."

I laughed at her. "You're forty-three, Kaiti. We both are. You're hardly over the hill just yet."

"Shhh!" She glared furiously at me. "You're forty-three, and in your prime. I'm forty-three and over the hill. Don't go confusing the two. You know it's different for us."

I chuckled again, amused. "This is nice. Why don't we do this more often?"

Kaiti shrugged. "I don't know. I mean, we're mature enough to be friends by now, surely?"

I nodded, drinking her in. No matter how many times I'd tried to tell myself that our break-up had been mutual and the best thing for the both of us, it had never rung true. Not in my heart. It never had. "Yeah, I'd like that," I said before I directed the conversation to focusing on her parents and her work.

By the end of it, my impromptu lunch with my ex-wife was one of the most enjoyable outings I'd had in a very long time.

CHAPTER 4

Patrick

New Year's Eve was at my cousin's place outside the city. I drove up every year and got to enjoy seeing the New Year surrounded by my family, good food, and too much wine.

This year however, everything felt different. With Chastity and I on the outs, and Kaiti and I... well, not on the outs anymore, I wasn't sure where I stood with either of them, and it was confusing as hell.

But I was a pro at hiding my real feelings, always had been. So, when my phone rang about eleven PM, I was already half a bottle of Jack Daniels in, and the music was pumping hard.

When I glanced down at the screen, I couldn't believe my eyes. "Excuse me for a sec," I said to one of my cousin's friends who'd been putting the moves on me since I first walked in. I marched toward the door that led to the patio so I could hear myself think and answered the phone. "What do you want?"

Axel laughed in an almost neurotic way I'd never heard before. "You picked up! I didn't think you would."

Oh my God. "Are you drunk?" Of course, he was. It was New Year's Eve. But I couldn't hear any music playing, nor any sounds except his breathing on the other end of the line.

After another few seconds he answered. "Yep. Are you?"

I pinched the bridge of my nose. Why the hell had I picked up the phone? "No." Though after this call I may need to finish the bottle of bourbon I'd started a few hours ago. "But I'm at a party, so I can't talk long. What do you want, Axel?" Surely, he wasn't just calling for an idle chat after everything?

"I want some advice."

"Advice?" I repeated, staring out into the darkness of the back yard. Since when did he do anything that I advised him to do? "From me?" *After what happened the other day?*

"Yeah. You know me better than anyone else, apparently," he slurred.

I clenched my jaw so hard I heard my teeth crack. *Shit.* I did know him, too well. "Ask. And make it quick." *This better be good.*

"Okay... so. You know how you told me to go for that girl I was into?"

Seriously? "I didn't mean—"

"You said that if I was finally interested in someone for more than a quick fuck, then I should pursue her, did you not?"

Of course, I fucking did! But that was when I thought he was dating someone suitable. And much closer to his own age! And bloody well not my only daughter! Finally, I had to admit. "Yes, I did. But I didn't know—"

"I know you didn't know it was your daughter, but the facts of the case haven't changed, so can I ask your advice again? Even though it didn't work out so well last time?"

I groaned because I couldn't yell at someone who was obviously too drunk to see reason anyway.

Axel continued as though I'd agreed to continue the conversation, "Okay. Well, the girl, the one I've been seeing for the last couple of weeks... we broke up. Again. And I cannot stop thinking about her."

I froze, not wanting to move or breathe or feel. Anything. This was not what I'd signed up for. *No way.*

Axel went on. "She's so different, Patrick, from anyone else I've ever met. She's sweet, but so fucking strong. She doesn't let me get away with anything, and we talk about everything together. She's smart, and funny, and..."

She was all those things, and so much more. So, despite the fact I wanted out of this conversation, something inside me forced out the words that would encourage him to keep talking. "And what?"

Axel sighed, long and heavily. "And compassionate and honest. I had a migraine the other night and didn't cancel our date. And you know what she did? She just sat on my bed and did this head massage thing until I fell asleep. I've never had anyone look after me before. Not my own mother, not anyone. Not ever! How does someone so young have such a big fucking heart?"

All the anger went out of me in one long rush, like someone had poked me with a safety pin and popped all the air around me. I walked over to one of the lounge chairs on the porch and sat down, elbows on my bent knees with my feet firmly planted on the floor. This conversation had just taken a turn for the worse.

"You still there?" Axel asked.

"Yeah," I said, even though I shouldn't be. "I'm still here."

"So, what do I do, Pat? I think I really hurt her when I didn't say I loved her back, and her dad fucking hates me."

I sighed, too many things rolling around in my head. After everything I'd seen, everything Kaiti had told me about how Chastity felt... could I really advise my best friend to act on his feelings? "You're an old man, Axel. She's at the beginning of her life. What are you going to offer her to make up for the twenty years of life she's missed out on with you?"

She'd never get to backpack through Europe or own an old, beat-up car that she paid for herself. She'd skip all the steps that made a person complete, and that was only if Axel and she even worked out. There was practically zero percent chance of that happening.

Then Axel said something that made my heart hurt. "I'll give her everything, Pat. Marriage. Babies. Houses all over the world. Whatever she wants."

I groaned. "Axel, don't fucking promise things you don't mean!" Because he seriously couldn't mean all that. It had to be the alcohol talking. My best friend had never even lived with a woman, not once. How did he think he was going to just slide on straight through to marriage? Just like that? Like it was easy?

"But I do mean it!" Axel yelled. "Don't you get it? She's the one I want! She's everything—and I'll wait for her. To finish college. Go to chiropractor school. Everything, if she wants that. She doesn't have to work."

"She'll want to work," I reminded him. We'd taught her better than that.

He laughed. "Yeah, I know. I can give her the world, and she wants to earn it herself. Kind of poetic, isn't it? The only woman who doesn't want me for my money."

Oh my God. He was serious. Axel wanted my daughter. *Holy hell. Will wonders never cease?* I frowned down at the phone. "I don't forgive you." *For being a lying scumbag.* That, I couldn't forgive. For loving my daughter? Well... I didn't really blame him.

"I know."

"And you have to convince Chasity of all that shit you just said, not me." I wasn't passing on that message, no way. She and I still had our own shit to sort out. She'd lied to me, and that had honestly hurt me more than Axel's betrayal.

"I know, Pat."

I took a deep breath. I couldn't believe I was agreeing to this. Kaiti would have a conniption if Axel became her son-in-law, but it was time for me to get out of the way. If they were going to build a relationship, or they were going to break up, it had to be because they'd made that decision; and not because I'd walked in on them fucking.

I couldn't be the reason my daughter wouldn't speak to me. But back to my best friend. "And if you ever, and I mean ever, lie to me again—"

"I won't," Axel rushed in to promise.

I huffed out the breath I'd been holding. "Okay, then."

"Okay, then... I can call her? Try and win her back?"

Yep. And good-fucking-luck. "You can try," I said, then remembered that she wasn't in the city. "But I'm not sure she's here anymore."

"What do you mean?" Axel asked. "She wasn't heading back to school until next week, was she?"

I sat back in the lounge chair, relaxing just a little. "Yeah, well, her mom said that she wasn't coping and wanted to head back early. So, I'm not sure if you wamt to brave an on-campus declaration of love, but you might have to, if you want her back."

"Her mom?" Axel repeated. "Are you two seeing each other again?"

Shit. How did Axel read me so well? No point lying. "We had lunch the other day. I don't know, man. Maybe too much water has gone under that bridge to start again." *Way too much water.* Twenty years' worth of arguments, money hassles, bad blood, and miscommunication. Not to mention the fact she still blamed me for our break-up, when she'd been the one who'd been impossible to live with.

"You're wrong," Axel said. "You two never really had your chance. The odds were stacked against you from the start."

He was right. We'd never had the chance to do so many things that we planned on. Travel. College. More kids. Getting pregnant with Chastity had changed the entire course of our lives. But were second chances real? Or were they just some made-up Hollywood movie bullshit?

"So, you think I should, you know... give it another go?" I asked hesitantly. Why I was asking Mr. Hit-it-and Quit-it, himself, I'd never know. But Axel knew me, better than almost anyone.

"Yeah, I do," he said. "After all, any woman who raised someone like Chastity can't be all bad. Right?"

My head hurt from all the truths being thrown at me. "I've got to go. Let me know how the groveling goes down." I got to my feet and started walking back inside the house. I needed a bottle of water, then it was time to start drinking again. I wasn't driving, after all.

Axel laughed loudly and even more drunkenly. "You'll probably see it on YouTube. It's going to be epic."

I hung up to stop Axel from hearing the cackle that started at the very idea of that.

The woman, Marie, who'd been flirting with me all night, sashayed up to the back door to smile at me. "Who was that?"

"Oh, just a friend of mine. He's..." How did I even begin to explain? "Planning on begging his ex-girlfriend to take him back and I just can't even imagine it."

"How come?" she asked, handing me a fresh drink.

I took it, because I needed it. "Because he's a player. In the best way.

He's just... not someone who ever wanted to settle down before now." And I couldn't see it happening. Not even for someone as remarkable as my daughter.

Marie shrugged. "Every girl wants a bad boy only she can tame."

Then her eyes slid sideways at me.

I took a sip of my bourbon, so that I wouldn't roll my eyes at her. "Let's get something to eat. I'm starving." And there wasn't enough liquor in the world to make me get into bed with someone like Marie.

I waited until midnight, avoiding a passionate kiss from Marie by just pecking her on the lips and swinging her around. Then I moved on to saying Happy New Year to all my family, and when Marie wasn't looking, I slipped away to the bedroom my cousin always reserved for me and locked the door.

I sent a quick text before I climbed into bed.

Happy New Year! Can we do lunch again? I have more news on the Axel front.

I stripped off and lay down on the pillow, my head spinning.

Kaiti texted straight back.

Happy New Year to you too. Yeah, sure. Noon at Dixie's?

I smiled.

Yep. See you in twelve hours.

I flung my arms out and closed my eyes. *What a strange way to start the year.*

CHAPTER 5
Katherine/Kaiti

I arrived at Dixie's early to order a good coffee. I'd been dying for one all morning, but I'd arranged to meet Patrick at noon, so I waited. My head was thumping with a brutal hangover headache, so I drank two glasses of icy water while I waited for my jumbo latte. And that's how Patrick found me; head in hands, wishing I'd stopped after a few glasses of wine like I'd originally planned.

"Good afternoon!" He greeted me, far too awake and bright for the day after New Year's.

I lifted my gaze to his smirking face and growled hopelessly at him. "How in God's name are you in such good health today?"

He laughed. "Good bourbon. How come you're in such bad shape?"

I groaned. "Cheap wine and too much of it."

The waiter arrived and served my coffee.

"Sorry, I went ahead and ordered," I apologized. "I needed the caffeine."

"Have you ordered food yet?" he asked, undaunted.

I shook my head and grabbed for the menu. Food... *eek*. I wasn't sure what my stomach could deal with after last night.

"Just order the big breakfast with me. It'll soak up the wine and I'll eat what you don't," Patrick offered.

"Sounds good," I said and pushed the menu away.

He called the waiter back and ordered for us.

A strange, squirmy feeling rose in the pit of my stomach. Sharing a meal was rather *intimate*. And finishing the rest of my food, like he did in the old days? I hadn't thought we were quite at that stage friendship-wise. *But it is economical*, I suppose. "So, you had a good night, then?" I asked, mostly to be polite. It was obvious he had.

"Yeah," he answered casually. "Just went to my cousin's and caught up with the family."

"Oh, Vinnie? How's he doing?" I asked. Vincent was the only cousin Patrick really liked, as far as I knew. Things may have changed, though.

But when Patrick grinned at me, I knew I'd guessed correctly. "He's good. He's married now with two kids."

"Married? God... I never thought that would happen," I admitted, before I stared down into my coffee and sighed. Everyone else had moved on with their lives and I felt like I was still doing the same thing I'd always done. Or had been doing anyway, for the last twenty-two years.

"Yeah. I suppose some things do change," he said.

I nodded. "For some of us."

Patrick tilted his head at me curiously but didn't pry.

Our food arrived and my stomach rolled at the smell of the greasy bacon and sausage.

"Just eat," Patrick commanded, watching me. "You'll feel better, trust me. The grease will do you good."

Trust him? I snorted but did as he suggested anyway. Starting with the toast and butter, I then moved on to the avocado and bacon. I probably managed to eat about half of everything, except the eggs, before pushing it toward Patrick. "You were right. That helped, but it's *way* too much."

Patrick, on the other hand, had already finished his own plate and now looked greedily at mine. "No problem," he said, putting my plate on top of his empty one, before bogging into mine as well.

I relaxed back against the chair and stared, simply soaking in the sight of him. For so many years, I'd been really angry with him. But now, feeling his naturally happy presence, I couldn't summon even a glimpse of the pain I'd once felt. "So, any news on Axel?" I asked, taking a long sip of my coffee and sighing as the caffeine infiltrated my bloodstream.

Patrick choked a little on his food, then bashed himself on the chest to clear his airway, as if taken by surprise. "Ah. Actually, yeah, I do." He coughed and spluttered some more.

I offered up his glass of water. I was busting to know, but waited until he got his breathing under control before, I asked again. "So, what's happened?"

"Nothing yet, I don't think. But Axel called me last night."

I wrapped my hands around my mug and gripped the porcelain tightly. "What did he say?"

Patrick sighed and ran his fingers through his dark hair.

I squeezed my mug even tighter. "Why do I feel like this is going to be bad?"

"It's not bad, Kaiti, but I've got to tell you what I said. You're going to be mad at me, probably, but I want to be honest with you."

I clenched my jaw for a moment, before unlocking it and forcing the words through my teeth. "Please do."

"Well, Axel called me, drunk as a skunk, and totally alone, at least if I was reading the sounds in the background correctly."

I shrugged. "And? Get to the good part."

"He apologized to me about lying to me."

"I hope you gave it to him about that." *I would have.* If the roles were reversed, Axel's ears would have been bleeding by the time I was done with him.

"I didn't punch him again, or anything but—"

"Again? What do you mean?" I balked.

He chuckled. "Didn't I tell you about that?"

I shook my head emphatically and laughed along as he told me all about how he'd punched Axel in the face after he'd broken up with Chastity.

I sighed happily at the imagery. "I only wish I'd been there to see it."

"You wouldn't have wanted to be there, believe me."

I smiled. "Yeah, I suppose so. But anyway, back to it."

"Okay, so long story short, he told me he loved her and wanted to go see her and beg for her forgiveness."

I gasped, my words sticking in my throat like shards of glass. When he didn't elaborate, I swallowed hard. "What did you say?"

Patrick shrugged. "What *could* I say? I told him that I didn't think he should do it, and I didn't think she'd forgive him, but if he wanted to try, I wouldn't stand in his way."

My hand flew up to my mouth as I covered my exasperated gasp. "Patrick!"

He shrugged again. "See? I knew you wouldn't like it."

"But... why? Why would you give him your blessing?"

He pushed himself back in his chair and crossed his arms over his chest. "Because he sounded so pathetic, so sorry, and so damn sad. I've never heard him like that before. There was no way I could say, 'No, you can't speak to her ever again.' What sort of man would that make me?"

A father! I almost yelled at him.

Patrick rolled his eyes. "Oh, stop it."

"Stop it?" I spluttered, rankled.

"Yeah, stop it. Chastity is twenty-two years old, and she has the right to knock him back herself. That's not my job. I'm not going to play gatekeeper of her happiness."

I stared at him, dumbstruck. "You think she'll knock him back?"

"I would," he snorted. "He's not exactly the marrying kind." His face suddenly flinched, then it smoothed out again.

I wasn't going to ask about that one. Instead, I put my hands up. "So let me get this straight. Axel called you, and you gave him permission to date our daughter?"

He stared at me, one brow raised. "I'm not the bad guy in all of this, Katherine. Please stop treating me like I am."

His use of my full name got me more than anything else could have. I took a sip of my water and forced myself to breathe, to not lose my shit in a public cafe.

"What are you really worried about?" he asked me suddenly. "What's the worst thing that could happen?"

"The worst thing?" I repeated. "She drops out of college and ends up pregnant and alone!"

There was a heavy beat of silence. "Was your life really that bad?" Patrick asked.

I groaned. "It was difficult, Patrick. And lonely. While you were off screwing Rochelle, I was raising a toddler on minimum wage."

Patrick's jaw tightened and anger flashed in his gaze.

I couldn't handle his expression, so I stared down at the table instead. "She deserves better than what I had, Patrick, that's all. Better than we both ended up with."

"No, don't change the subject," Patrick said. "We're going to talk about this once and for all."

I sat back and crossed my legs, swiveling to the side. "Talk about what?"

"That shit about Rochelle. We dated, yes, but not until *ages* after you and I broke up. She never moved in and Chastity never met her. In fact, I've never been serious enough about any of my girlfriends to introduce them to Chastity."

I knew that in regard to her later years in his care, but in earlier times, how would I know who slept near my daughter? "It doesn't matter now," I muttered.

Patrick put both hands down flat onto the table and stared at me. "It does matter. You seem to think I did wrong by you. I didn't. You were the one who left."

"Because you were seeing Rochelle!" I yelled back at him. *Damn it.* I really didn't want to lose my cool.

"No, I wasn't," he responded evenly.

"Yes, you were. She told me you two had been dating in secret for months before we split up." I choked on the words as they passed my lips, but it was good to finally get them out. It was a relief, like expelling venom from my life that had been poisoning my veins for far too long. At the time, I'd been furious to think he'd cheated on me. But the truth was we'd been on the rocks basically ever since Chastity was born, so I hadn't been truly surprised.

But from the look on Patrick's face, he was shocked. "Are you telling me that you think I cheated on you?"

I nodded and grimaced. "I didn't know until after you left, of course, but Rochelle told me later on just how long you two had been together and how much time she spent with Chastity." She used to quote little personal things about my daughter that only someone very close to Patrick would know, so, naturally, I'd had no reason to doubt her words.

"That bitch!" Patrick growled, his hands tightening into fists on top of the table. "I cannot believe—"

I shrugged. "It was a long time ago now and I know I wasn't the easiest to deal with." I'd had a pretty severe case of undiagnosed post-natal depression and hadn't made anything easy on Patrick. Looking back, I could see it. But at the time, when I was deep inside that down-ward spiral of sleep deprivation and depression, well... Patrick's feelings had been the last thing on my mind.

Patrick leaned forward, catching my eye and holding my gaze. "Listen to me, Kaiti. I never, and I mean *never* cheated on you. It was a month after you kicked me out that I finally let Rochelle take me out on a date. I didn't want to, but she'd told me she'd seen you out with some guy, and I just assumed you'd moved on."

My mouth dropped open. "You believed her?"

He stared me down. "You believed her!"

"You two got together," I reminded him. "For years!" And they'd been terrible years too. I'd been twenty-four, with a two-year-old, and separated. Then, quickly divorced. It had been a whirlwind of pain and regret.

"Because you didn't want me," Patrick bit back at me. "You told me often enough."

I shuffled on my seat. "Are you telling me that Rochelle made all that shit up?"

"I'm telling you that she never met our daughter and I only started seeing her *after* I was sure you were done with me."

My heart screamed out in pain and rage and disbelief. And before I could stop it a whisper floated my lips. "I was never done with you, Patrick."

He heard me, because I saw the recognition register in his eyes.

"Then why..." He shook his head, then reached over the table to hold my hand.

I turned my wrist instinctively and let him interlink our fingers together. I stared at our hands for far too long, but it didn't matter. There was nothing more to say now.

We'd been driven apart by stress and stupidity and kept apart by naivety and bitchiness. *At least Rochelle never got him long-term*, I thought. Because she wouldn't have been a good wife, and she was never a great friend.

Patrick deserved someone who could make him smile and laugh. Someone who knew what sort of person he truly was and was prepared to nurture that beautiful, giving soul of his.

CHAPTER 6

Patrick

The next day, I was at home on the computer, still reeling from yesterday's revelations, and getting prepared to go back to work, when my phone rang. I stared down at the screen and sucked in a deep breath. "Oh, shit." I shook myself, preparing for the worst. "Chastity," I said carefully.

"Hey, Dad."

The sound of her voice was happy and relaxed, and it sent such a wave of relief through me that I was glad I was already sitting down. The big question was though, was she calling just to chat—to resolve things between us—or had Axel already made the trip down to her school? Had they made up or gotten into a big fight? *What could have possibly gone down?*

Too much time and silence passed since our greeting, so I jumped in with the first thing I could think of. "I missed not having you here for New Year's."

Not that she would have come to Vinnie's, but I'd always caught up with her around that time. I genuinely missed having her home, full stop.

"Yeah... I wish I'd been there too, Dad. I hope you understood why I left."

I sighed and leaned back into my desk chair. "I did and I do. Breaking up is hard." Not to mention the fallout from me finding her with my best friend, unclothed at that. But I wasn't bringing that up again if I could help it.

"Yeah, it was. And my first break-up."

Her first a lot of things. "Have you heard from Axel since then?" I asked, trying to keep my tone casual and failing miserably.

"Yeah, he came by school yesterday."

"He came by?" I repeated. "How?"

She laughed. "What do you mean, how? He drove. He actually came into the college grounds and found me at the library, but the librarian refused to let him in! She made him wait outside."

I laughed at the mental image. Axel being treated like a regular Joe. I never would have thought I'd see the day. *Brilliant.* "Axel was refused entry into a library? Oh, I would liked to have been there to see that."

He'd never been refused entry, anywhere that I was aware of—he was a billionaire for Christ's sake. It would have been great to see him eating some humble pie for once.

Chastity chuckled. "Yeah, it was sort of awesome."

I wanted to fist pump the air. *That's my girl.* So, had she sent him packing? Had he begged? Had she taken him back? Curiosity was eating me alive. "So... what happened?"

She went silent for a minute.

I pressed the phone harder into my ear.

"Well... we got back together."

Oh, God. Kaiti is going to kill me.

"Dad?"

"I'm here, sweetheart. Did you two manage to sort everything out?" I pressed my fingers into my forehead, an instant headache developing there.

"Yeah, we did. Well, as much as we could. I was worried about you and how you felt about us and everything. But Axel assured me that you'd given him permission to come and apologize."

Oh, shit. Please let that not be the only reason they're back together. "I did. And I'm glad he apologized for being a dick. But tell me... how does a billionaire say I'm sorry? I've never heard those words cross Axel's lips." I stood up and pushed away from my desk, unable to stay seated while my world shifted on its axis once more. I'd just gotten over the idea that my daughter and my best friend had been together briefly. Now... *shit*.

"Well," she began, "he did say he was sorry, multiple times. And he bought me some things to make dating each other easier. You know, with the whole long-distance thing."

I narrowed my eyes. That sounded like Axel. Throw money at a problem and see if it stuck. "What kind of things did he buy you?" I asked.

"Well, he got me a car."

"A car! What kind?" I gasped.

"A Beetle."

My jaw clamped down and my teeth clicked together. *So much for her learning the value of earning herself a car.* "What else?" Because that wouldn't be the end of the list. If Axel wanted something, he went after it, no holds barred. Something I hadn't really considered when it had come to Chastity. I'd assumed, of course, that she'd put him in his place. Or at least see there was no real future for them.

"Well, the second thing isn't for me, so to speak..." She paused for a moment.

The breathless moment made my heart sink. What had he done?

"But he bought an apartment about five minutes from here, so he can stay when he comes for weekends. And he said you or Mom can come stay too. It has three bedrooms."

I exhaled through my nose, my teeth too tightly clamped together to speak. He'd bought her—*them*— a love nest?

"Dad?" Chastity pressed. "Are you okay?"

I closed my eyes, willing the anger away. "Just be careful, baby, okay? I love Axel, but his track record with dating is shit. He's not really good boyfriend material, and I want only good things for you. I don't want you to get hurt again." And a month or two of dating a player wasn't on the list of good things. But she was an adult, and so was he, so I had to step away. For today, anyway.

"I know, Dad. Thank you. And I'm really sorry about everything."

"You mean the part where you dated my best friend behind my back or the lying to me?" I snarked without thinking. *Aw, crap. Fucking good one, Patrick.* Well, it was out there now.

"Yeah. All of that, Dad. I'm *so* sorry. I never wanted to hurt you."

All the anger I'd been holding evaporated with her words. I didn't want the relationship I had with my daughter destroyed, so I was going to have to let this go. At least when I spoke to Chastity about it. Axel and I on the other hand were an entirely different matter.

"I know, baby. Okay." I inhaled, then released my breath in a sigh. "Thank you for telling me you two are back together. I want things between us to remain honest."

"No problem, Dad."

It had better not be a problem. She only had a few months left before graduation. He better not screw any of it up. "Anyway, I better go, Chastity. We'll talk during the week sometime, okay?" I closed my eyes and held my breath again, not wanting to give away just how annoyed I was still.

"Sure! Thanks, Dad," she said and hung up.

I threw my phone onto the couch before I could punch it through a wall. *Holy shit. What a mess!* Kaiti was going to have a cow.

But if I'd learned anything from any of this, it's that there was no time like the present, and being truthful. *I should tell her before Chastity does, so she'll be prepared.* Hopefully. I picked up my phone and called her, a woman I'd spoken to more in the past week that I had in the past twenty years.

"Hey, Patrick. How are you?" she answered quickly, which was pleasing.

Um... "Uh... I'm not sure."

"What do you mean?" she asked, her tone immediately sharp.

I began to pace, preparing myself mentally for the barrage of abuse to follow once I shared the news. "Well, I just got word from Chastity that she and Axel are back together again."

CHAPTER 7

Katherine/Kaiti

"What?" I gasped, my face paling. "But we thought she'd tell him to go to Hell!" That, and I'd really hoped that Chastity would finally realize that there was no future with a man like Axel. Sure, he'd be a ton of fun short-term, but my daughter wasn't one of those types of girls who knew how to 'just have fun'; feelings were going to get hurt!

Truthfully, I never had been either. I still wasn't. Once I fell, I fell hard. *And apparently never recovered,* I mused. Hence, my singledom. I slumped down onto the couch, folding my laundry forgotten. "How did this happen? Or don't I want to know?" Axel was the sort of guy that could have seduced her right back into his bed, that or he'd just thrown money at the problem, I was sure of it.

"I don't have any details," Patrick went on to say. "As in, nothing salacious at least. But she called me just now to apologize for everything, and to tell me they'd gotten back together."

I stared up at the ceiling, trying to stop the stubborn, angry tears that gathered in my eyes, threatening to spill. "This wasn't supposed to happen, Patrick."

"I know," he said softly. "But look, Axel is a workaholic, the worst

40

I've ever met. There's no way a relationship between them is going to work in the long run."

"But what about the short-term?" I burst out at the intrepid consolation. "She has studies! Exams!" I couldn't see my daughter make the same mistake I had. I couldn't. She deserved so much more. *We taught her so much better than this!* I thought with deflated frustration.

"Exactly!" Patrick said. "She has a full-time course load and lives two hours away. He works a hundred hours a week and prioritizes work over everything else. How do you think that's going to go?"

I sank deeper into the couch and sighed, mulling the thought over from an object point of view. "Not well I imagine."

"No, it's not. Long distance relationships are difficult for anyone, and they've only known each other a month. There's no way they'll last," Patrick assured me.

I lay down on the couch and pressed a hand to my forehead, feeling for the first time utterly powerless in helping my daughter navigate her life. How had it gone from carefree to complicated so fast? My head was spinning. "So, what do you suggest then?" I asked Patrick, because I had no clue how to proceed from here.

"We do nothing."

"Nothing!" I exclaimed, gesticulating to the ceiling above me.

Patrick sighed. "Do you remember how long it took you and your mom to get back to talking terms after we got married?"

I pressed my lips together, hard. "What's your point?"

"My point is, you don't want to let Axel drive a wedge between Chastity and either of us. He might only last a month, and yet the damage this could cause longterm to our relationships with Chastity might become irreparable."

He has a point. "Okay, so we just support the fact they're back together and leave her to it? Just play happy families as long as it lasts?" I asked, massaging my brow to relieve the pressure building there.

"Yeah, why not?" said Patrick. "She's never confided in us about dating before and she's managed her schooling and schedule just fine. I'm sure, ultimately, she'll figure all this out too."

I rolled my eyes and pulled myself up to sit on the couch again. *She's never had to manage it before because she's never really dated anyone!* A serious, long-term relationship with a man twice her age? That was going to take some serious juggling, and I wasn't sure Chastity was up to the task. "I just don't want her to ruin her life, Patrick. We've worked too hard to get her to this point."

And by we, I meant both Patrick and me. We'd supported her financially through high school and college the best we could, never wanting for her to stress about working too much outside of classes. We wanted better for her than what we ever had.

"She'll be okay, Kaiti. You raised a good girl."

I sniffed, then wiped my nose with a nearby tissue. "We both did, Patrick."

There was a long silence, then he sighed. "All right, well, I better get back to work. But I'll chat with you soon?"

I smiled, liking the sound of that. "Sure. Thanks for calling right away. I appreciate the heads up."

"You're welcome. Bye." Patrick hung up and my phone dinged immediately.

Axel and I talked and sorted everything out.

It was a text from Chastity.

I rolled my eyes. Patrick got some long, in-depth conversation and I got a text? *Lovely.*

I'm glad, honey. As long as you're happy. And if you need to talk, call anytime.

I forced myself to reply back.

The next message that came through was a picture of Chastity, grinning her head off, inside a car.

Oh! And he bought me a car so that I can drive up and down on the weekends. How cool is that?

I growled aloud at that one. *Ugh!* He was buying her expensive, unnecessary gifts now? Of course, he was. At least it was more useful than the diamond necklace she got for Christmas.

Your first car should be one you work for and buy yourself.

I texted back before I thought better about it.

Sorry, Mom.

I put the phone down and pressed my face into my hands, my shoulders slumped. I was still driving around in the car I'd bought twenty years ago after I had Chastity; and Axel had bought her a brand new one just like that? I blew out a long breath and forced myself to concentrate. *Patrick was right.* If I wasn't careful, I'd destroy my relationship with my daughter, and that was the last thing in the world I wanted.

It's okay, honey. You're just very lucky.

I answered.

Bye.

She replied.

Bye xox.

I got up and went back to folding the laundry, my arms shaking with a newfound tension and anger I couldn't even begin to explain. This was not going to end well. I felt it in my bones.

CHAPTER 8

Katherine/Kaiti

Somehow, between work and life, Patrick and I went out for a second lunch, and then a third. Then he texted to ask me if I wanted to go on a "real date," and I almost fell over.

A real date? Was he insane? I'd justified every lunch up until this point by telling myself that they were for Chastity's benefit. That we were simply meeting as co-parents, who had finally grown up enough to have a friendship after divorce.

And we *did* talk about Chastity, for some of the lunch. For at least the first ten minutes, anyway...

I'm not sure if we should.

I texted him.

He didn't bother arguing with me and replied instantly.

Friday night, 7pm. Ballagios.

I squealed—loudly—Like some stupid schoolgirl with a teenage crush. Then it dawned on me, Friday night was tomorrow night! *Holy shit.* I texted back before I could talk myself out of it. At this point in my life, after spending half of my adult life without a partner, what did I really have to lose?

Okay. See you then.

I put my hand over my mouth, stifling any more noise. This was an insane thing to do. But I wanted to do it! Lunch with Patrick last weekend had taught me that everything we'd both believed about our break-up all these lonely years had been manipulated by Rochelle. My ex-friend and his ex-girlfriend.

She'd convinced me that Patrick had cheated on me, and that she was a permanent fixture in his life and Chastity's. Which, looking back, had truly been the final nail in the coffin of our relationship. The sting of being replaced so easily and heartlessly was too much to bear in the end.

With all of the stress, anxiety, and pressure of those apparent secrets simmering in the background, we'd broken up one night over some stupid fight. The weight of it all triggering me. That little spat was the proverbial straw that broke the camel's back. But truthfully, despite the pain and the break-up, I'd spent months secretly hoping and waiting for him to come back to us—his family. But he hadn't.

And now I knew it was because Rochelle had been manipulating the both of us, pulling the strings behind the curtains like we were her puppets in some sick power play of hers. But did that mean that we really could have made it all along? And did that then mean we had a chance of making it work this time? Was Patrick even looking for a relationship? I had no real clue.

Or was all of this nothing more than a trip down memory lane for him? Because if he was looking to refresh his memory, my body looked *nothing* like it did when we were married. There was a world of difference between twenty-one and forty-three. A ridiculous amount of time had passed under that bridge. And if he had any notions of rekindling where we left off, he was going to be sorely disappointed.

I was tired and over-worked. My trial by fire had been a tough one. I wasn't as fresh as a spring daisy anymore. *But what if he wants something real?* A voice in the back of my mind whispered. Biting my lower lip, I teased it between my teeth in thought, past regrets bubbling just below the surface. Was I willing to take that second chance? Or was I jumping in the deep end with romantic blinkers on and setting myself up for more hurt?

There's only one way to find out.

CHAPTER 9

Patrick

I was at work on Friday when my phone rang. Chastity's name flashed up on the screen, so I picked up straight away. "Hey, sweetheart. This is a surprise."

"Hey, Dad! Yeah... well, I have another surprise for you. I'm driving down this weekend and was wondering if I could crash at your place tonight? No stress if you have plans to go out or anything, I'll just study and get an early night."

Oh, crap! Of all the nights for her to come to town and want to spend the night, it had to be tonight. My first proper date with Kaiti after all these years. "Ah... yeah. Okay, sure."

"It's fine if you can't, Dad. I'll figure something out."

"No!" I said, thinking quickly. "I want to see you, and you can come. I already had dinner plans, so if you're okay with me going out for a couple of hours..." I was meeting Kaiti at seven PM, so if all went well, a ten PM finish would be pretty feasible. If things went south, well, I'd be home early.

"Yeah, of course I am. Like I said, I have a ton of studying to do. You do whatever you've got to do, Dad."

I smiled to myself. That was my girl. Keeping up with her studies, making us proud. "Then, if you don't mind me asking, how come the surprise trip if you have a lot of work to do?" It didn't really make sense. Even though her school wasn't far from us, she rarely visited during the semester. Didn't visit me, anyway.

"Axel has a work dinner tomorrow night and asked me to join him. And since we didn't really get to say goodbye properly last week, I thought we could spend tonight together and then go out for breakfast, maybe?"

He... *what?* Axel had invited her to meet work contacts? That meant that he really was serious about her! Much more so than I'd ever anticipated. I spoke slowly, so as to not alert her to how panicked my heart had just become. "A work dinner? You're going to a work dinner with him?"

"Yeah. Why's that, Dad? Is that bad?" Chastity asked.

"Oh, no," I reassured her. "It's not that. Just... I'm distracted, sorry, sweetheart. Don't worry about it. I'll see you when you get here. You've got your key, still, right?" This was bad. Kaiti was going to freak. Chastity's and Axel's relationship was escalating at a record pace!

"I do."

I forced a smile to my face so that I sounded happy. "Well, I'll see you at home, then. There's food in the fridge and some cash in the fruit bowl if you want to order something in, okay?"

"Thanks, Dad," she said, warmth filling her voice.

"See you soon!" I said and hung up. "Oh, shit." Axel was super serious about Chastity for real. And now I was dating her mother again...

More was happening in this family at the moment than had gone on in the past twenty years. It was mind-boggling and I wasn't quite sure how any of us were going to get out of this unscathed. Was this entire situation going to crash or burn? Or could we really all get our impossible Happily Ever Afters?

I turned back to my computer and got back to work. Only time would tell what the outcome would be in the end, but I had hope that everything would work out. And sometimes, hope was all we ever had; a hope, a wing, and a prayer. So, for now, it would have to be enough.

CHAPTER 10

Katherine / Kaiti

I pushed through the tension and anxiety of what would happen to us if everything went to shit, but regardless of my misgivings Friday night rolled around and it was time to confront my fears. It was seven PM, and I was dolled up for the first time in as long as I could remember. With a face full of war paint on and my hair blow dried out fashionably, things were as good as they were going to get.

When I walked into the restaurant, I scanned the area with my eyes, keeping my breathing as even and calm as I could manage.

Patrick was already standing by the concierge desk, staring at me.

I paused on the spot, my belly trembling at the sight of him.

His gaze ate me up, running down my body, all the way to my toes, then flicking back up to my face again.

I sucked in my stomach, put on a smile, and walked over on unsteady legs toward him. "Hey."

"Hey, yourself" he said, sliding his hand instantly around my waist. "You look beautiful."

And I felt beautiful. I always had when Patrick looked at me like that. "Thank you. You look very handsome too." And he did. With crisp, black dress shirt and black slacks, his strong body was only accentuated by the way the material of the sleeves clung to the chiseled muscles of his arms.

"Let's go in," he whispered into my ear, his breath warm on my cheek.

I shivered at the sensation, then walked with him behind the maître d' to a table in the back of the restaurant. We were seated and ordered wine before we were left to quietly stare at each other.

"So..." I began.

"So..." Patrick repeated, then grinned at me. "How's work for you at the moment?"

I shrugged noncommittally. "It's okay, I guess. You know, it pays the bills."

Patrick sighed and nodded. "Yeah, I know *exactly* what you mean."

I frowned at him, my brow quirked. "What do you mean? I thought you loved your job."

He grinned at me. "And how would you know that considering we haven't spoken about anything remotely personal in twenty years?"

Heat blazed in my cheeks, but I didn't look away. The waiter approached and served our wine, giving me time to form a more feasible response than I occasionally gave into curiosity and nostalgia and stalked him on social media. "Chastity would talk about you on occasion," I said, picking up my glass. "And I suppose I assumed that you were happy."

He shrugged again but didn't say anything.

It looked like the onus was on me to carry forward the conversation. "So, are you happy, Patrick? With your work?"

"Not really," he finally answered with a sigh. "I mean, yeah, it pays the bills. I've been able to pay off my apartment, help Chastity through college, but it isn't the most stimulating job in the world. It's just a means to an end, really."

I swallowed hard, a tightness beginning to grip me in the throat. "What about the rest of your life? Socially, personally? Are you happy?"

He stared directly at me this time. "Come on, we're too old for games, Kaiti. What are you really asking?"

I opened my mouth, then shut it again. Took a slug of my wine and swallowed it down mechanically. I had to think about this properly, and

I couldn't ask some stupid, offhand question. Tonight was special. It was going to determine a lot of our future. I could feel the power of change in the air.

Patrick was watching me, waiting. Which said a lot about his perspective. He wanted to see what I wanted and how I felt. Perhaps only then would he reveal his own intentions.

After a moment, I took a deep breath and opened the walls around my heart— just a crack. "I'm asking if you're happy with your life, Patrick? With how it turned out?"

"You mean, would I do things differently if I could go back in time?" he countered.

I offered him a small smile and nodded. "Yeah. Do you regret anything?" I know I certainly did.

Patrick inhaled sharply. "I regret letting Rochelle convince me that you didn't want me anymore. I regret letting age and lack of experience, not to mention stupidity, break up our family," he said, his tone one of searing honesty.

"You never remarried again," I whispered. "Why?"

"Why didn't you?" he countered again.

Part of me wanted him to answer first, of course. But that was the cowardly side of me. Now was the time for bravery. I had to lay all my cards out on the table. "That's easy," I answered, taking another sip of wine. "I never met anyone who I trusted with Chastity the way I trusted you."

He glanced down at the menu as if a little disappointed. "Any other reason?"

My heart screamed out at me not to expose myself. It reminded me that I'd been hurt before, and it just wasn't worth the risk, again. But I had to do it. This might be the only chance I would ever have to find out if Patrick and I had the opportunity of a real second chance. "Yes," I began, then took another fortifying sip of my wine. "I never loved anyone the way I loved you." When I finally glanced up to look at Patrick's face, his eyes were alight with a passion I hadn't seen in too many years to count. I fiddled with the white tablecloth. "What about you?"

"You were the love of my life, Kaiti. I couldn't replace you in my life or my heart. I didn't even try."

His words made tears gather in my eyes. *So many wasted years apart.* "Ah…" I wasn't even sure what I was going to say next.

The waiter came along, his timing impeccable, and took our orders. "Would you like to look at a dessert menu?" he asked.

I glanced at Patrick.

His face fell. "I have to go after dinner," he explained. "Chastity called today to say she's coming down for the weekend and asked if she could stay at my place."

My stomach sank with the weight of a lead balloon. "She didn't tell me she was coming up for the weekend."

Patrick dismissed the waiter and turned his focus back to me. "She's only staying with me because Axel's busy working tonight. They're supposed to be catching up tomorrow for the rest of the weekend."

I glanced down at the pristine white place setting. Chastity had always preferred to stay with me over her dad. They'd always had a great relationship, but being her custodial parent meant that she generally stayed in my house. Being second choice for once hurt more than I expected it would.

"I'm sorry I didn't tell you earlier, Kaiti," Patrick said. "But I didn't want tonight to be about Chastity."

I inhaled abruptly and pulled my gaze up to his once more. "I know, it's okay, honestly. It just hurts a bit, that's all."

Chastity and I still weren't good, that much was now clear. Thanks to her relationship with Axel, we might not be for a long time to come. But we'd always been close, and I knew things would come back around to how they were meant to be when the time was right.

"Yeah, I know."

I shook myself out of my mommy-self-pity trip and forced a smile. "Let's get back to what we were talking about, because you're right. We've spent twenty-two years talking about Chastity. We've probably earned a break."

Patrick laughed and it was a deep, solid sound. "You're right. So, what else do you want to talk about?"

I changed the subject to his family, then work, and travel, steering away from the super serious topics that the night had begun with. It was clear we felt the same way about each other, but I'd wait until the time was right to act on it.

That time, it seemed, was about an hour later, when we were walking out of the restaurant.

Patrick's hand slid into mine, intertwining our fingers as we walked along. "Where's your car?" he asked.

I pointed down the street. "A block that way."

"I'll walk you." And he did. He walked beside me in silence, just holding my hand like we were back in high school, and the world still held limitless possibilities.

"This is me," I said to break the silence enfolding us like a magic spell.

He nodded, then pushed me back until I was pressed against my car, his body hot against mine. "Can I kiss you goodnight, Kaiti?" he asked.

My heart immediately leapt into my throat, and I nodded, because what other possible answer was there?

He leaned in and waited, his lips a mere inch away. His dark eyes were locked with mine, their intensity palpable.

I couldn't breathe. Feelings I'd long forgotten and thought dead curled to life inside me, hot and aching with need. I couldn't wait any longer. I slid my hands up his arms and dug my nails into his huge biceps, welcoming the intimacy.

His lips met mine, startling moans out of the both of us.

I melted into him, gliding my fingers up into his hair and grabbing the back of his skull. Then I pulled him into me as tight as he would come, fitting him against me like a long-lost jigsaw piece.

His arms wrapped around my body and our lips parted, letting our tongues dance like they'd never been apart. The kiss went on and on, with Patrick's familiar hands pressing into my back, my waist, my ass, until finally, he pulled back ever so slightly.

I stumbled against him; passion dazed.

He held me up with his strong arms, supporting me, as if it were the most natural thing in the world to do. As if twenty-two years hadn't passed between us.

I pushed my ass back against the car, so I didn't weigh him down.

"Whoa," I breathed. I shouldn't have said it, but once it was out there, there was no taking it back again.

He nodded, his breathing heavy, then leaned forward to press his forehead to mine. "I wholeheartedly agree. *Whoa*."

I closed my eyes and stayed that way for too long, not caring who might walk past, who might see us. I only cared that after so long, we were finally in each other's arms once more. It felt so right that it took my breath away.

Then he pulled back, groaning. "I wish I didn't have to go, Kaiti. I'm sorry."

A smile trembled on my lips as he pulled away. Cold air filled the space where his hot body had been, and I wrapped my arms around my middle to warm myself again. I felt his absence acutely. "I understand, you have to go." Then I grinned at him. "Our daughter is waiting for you."

He looked torn, which I appreciated. It made me feel wanted and my heart swelled after years of neglect and loneliness. "It's okay, Patrick. Go."

He stepped into me, pressing his hard body against mine. "I'm sure you can *feel* just how much I wish I could take you home," he whispered.

I nodded, closing my eyes against the huge wave of arousal that swept over my touch-starved body. Patrick's cock was thick and hard, and pressing into my belly.

He gripped my chin with his fingers and tilted my head up, so I was forced to look at him.

I opened my eyes even though part of me was terrified of what would happen next. Everything had gone *too* perfectly so far, and I really couldn't believe it. I was scared the illusion might break, shattering like glass at my feet.

"Look at me," he commanded. "When we make love again, for the first time, I don't want to be rushed. I want to make you scream my name over and over and show you just how much I want us to be together."

I nodded and pressed my lips together, swallowing the moan of pleasure his words evoked. How much did he want us to be together? It looked like I'd have to wait and see. "Okay, Patrick."

He dropped another hot, fast kiss on my lips, then stepped away once more. "I'll see you soon, yeah?"

I nodded, running my tongue over my lips to absorb his taste. "Okay."

Then he turned and jogged away, into the dark of night.

I stayed there, half slumped against my car, half dazed, just staring after him as he ran off with a part of my heart I'd never really reclaimed. *God, what have I just done?*

CHAPTER 11

Patrick

Walking away from Kaiti in that moment of rekindled passion was one of the hardest things I'd had to do in my life, and I'd done a lot of hard things over the years. But looking down at her, seeing her eyes full of love and hope, and telling her I couldn't take her to bed when we both clearly wanted it so badly… *Fuck.* Yeah. Not fun.

But I told myself that our time would come. I didn't want to be stressed or rushed, nor be thinking about our troubles with Chastity. When I finally made love to Kaiti again, it would be in a comfortable bed with nights and days stretched out ahead of us. I'd make sure we had the gift of time to properly immerse ourselves in our newfound second chance. And the days and nights we'd have together would be filled with nothing but passion.

When I got back to my apartment, my blood had finally cooled down from what was definitely one of the best and most immersive kisses of my life. With a final conscious thought I took a deep breath to settle myself completely before entering my home. I plastered a smile on my face. "Hey, sweetheart!" I called out to my daughter.

"Hey, Dad!" Chastity answered. She sounded happy, which was always a bonus.

I walked into my living room and there she was, sitting on the couch in her pajamas like nothing had changed. If she wasn't so grown up, I could almost envisage my little blonde-haired girl just relaxing and snacking while watching cartoons, like she used to when she was a kid. "How was your night?" I asked her.

"Quiet but good. How was yours?

I put my keys down on the counter and ran a hand through my hair. "Yeah… good, too, thanks." It had been so much better than I'd thought it would be, and my expectations had been pretty high going in to be honest. My heart longed for Kaiti.

"Hot date?" she asked with an impish grin.

I froze. I wasn't ready to share this with Chastity, not yet. The romance between her mother and I was just blossoming again. I wanted to give it time to grow before we went announcing anything official or solid. "Yeah, sort of," I admitted vaguely.

She frowned. "You look nervous. What's wrong, Dad?"

I shook myself. *Stop acting like you're guilty of something! You've done nothing wrong,* I chastised myself. "Nothing's wrong, sweetheart. I'm just not ready to talk about it, that's all. It's too new." *Too old, was more like it.*

She tilted her head and stared at me like she could see every secret I held back. "I never really understood that expression," she said. "Do you mean it's too early to tell if it's going to last?"

I scratched my chin, then licked my lips. "Yeah, pretty much."

She sighed. "I think that's a bit of a cop-out."

"Oh, yeah?" I asked, crossing my arms over my chest and quirking a brow. "You're an expert on relationships now, are you?" Because as far as I knew, having one boyfriend hardly beat me out for experience.

She laughed. "Hardly. I don't know, I guess I just always figured that you could tell within an hour or two with most people as to whether you're going to be friends or not. And the same applies to romantic relationships. So? Do you like her?"

I nodded, feeling deflated by my daughter's no-nonsense approach to everything. "Yeah, I do. So, I suppose I'm just nervous of messing it up." Which was the understatement of the century. The stakes were too high in this arena. Too many people stood to get hurt if things went awry; including the young woman who sat in front of me.

"I get that," she admitted, chewing on her lip while she was thinking. "Dad… did you ever want to get married again? Have more kids?"

"Huh?" I said, bending my head to run a hand through my hair. I didn't want to have this conversation. Not now. "What's with the third degree, Chastity?"

"Sorry!" she said, jumping up from the couch. "I didn't mean for it to sound like an interrogation. It's just that, well, since being with Axel, it's made me think more about life and relationships. And you and Mom."

"What about us?" I asked, frowning at her.

Kaiti and I weren't Chastity's business. In our own ways, we'd stayed single to protect her. To give her as stable and as loving an environment as we could, considering we were divorced. Why was she questioning all those decisions now, especially with so much time and water under the bridge?

She slapped her hand against her forehead and grimaced. "Shit. This conversation isn't going well at all. Let's start again! Dad, how was your day?"

Guilt assailed me. I didn't want my only daughter to feel like she couldn't ask questions or talk to me. "No," I said, dropping my arms down. "It's okay. We can continue the conversation. So, why are you worried about your mom and me all of a sudden?" The topic had never really come up before, it was just a little odd that she was asking now and out of the blue. Did she know something about us? Had Axel perhaps said something to her?

Chastity shrugged. "Because I've just realized that I'm almost twenty-two, and neither of my parents ever re-married. And I suppose I'm just worried that it's my fault that you missed out on having more kids or getting married again. I feel like maybe I prevented you both from finding happiness again? I don't know." She suddenly covered her face with her hands. "I'm sorry, it's just—"

Sadness hit me hard and fast, along with a nice big dose of guilt. Here I was, worried about why Chastity was giving me the third degree and she was in tears over what she could have done differently when she was the child, and I was the adult.

Pull yourself together, man. Your daughter needs your assurance! I went over and grabbed her arms, squeezing her biceps gently. "Hey. Look at me."

She dropped her arms with a defeated expression and looked up at me with tear-filled eyes. "What?"

I smiled at her, willing my love for her into my eyes. "I never regretted the choice we made to have you, sweetheart. Perhaps I could have gotten married and had other children, maybe... I'll never know. It obviously wasn't on the cards for me. But none of that changes the fact that I love you. Okay? You have been nothing but a source of happiness for both your mother and I."

In the dark hours, over the years, I'd often wondered how things might have been different for me, especially when I was single and lonely. If we hadn't gotten pregnant when we did, would Kaiti and I have ultimately stayed together? Would we have traveled and tied the knot later? Would we have gone on to have two, three, or even four kids together? Or would we have broken up anyway? Would I have met someone else? It was pointless to ponder, really. The past was the past and couldn't be changed. Not now, not ever.

Chastity nodded. "Okay, Dad, but don't you ever—"

"No, I don't," I stressed. "I have a great life, and a daughter I'm very proud of." That part was very true.

Chastity smiled but her chin trembled. "Okay, Dad."

"Good girl," I said, then walked toward the kitchen. This situation definitely called for junk food. "Let's break out the chocolate stash I kept from Christmas," I suggested.

She laughed, probably surprised I had chocolate hidden in my apartment. "That sounds great."

So, for what remained of the night, we ate chocolate until we both felt sick, watched TV, and talked together.

When she eventually went to bed, I took a shower and climbed into my own bed, pulling out my cell phone to text Kaiti. She hadn't sent one, which didn't surprise me. She'd probably be worried that Chastity might see the notification.

Thanks for tonight, Kaiti. Best dinner I've had in twenty years.

She wrote back within a moment.

LOL. Yeah... for me too, Patrick.

I grinned, lying on my bed, sighing like a teenager in love for the first time all over again. It felt like DeJa'Vu. I had to see her again.

Do you want to go out for dinner again Tomorrow night? Or we could do take-out and a movie at my place?

I sent the message and held my breath. Kaiti liked to eat out. It was a luxury for her, and I understood that. We'd both struggled for money for a long time, and I wouldn't begrudge her a proper date night if that's what she had her heart set on.

The text she shot back took an extra minute or two to arrive, as though she were mulling it over.

Maybe we should book dinner at the Raddisson?

I laughed. *Oh, yeah.* The Radisson had a nice boutique restaurant, but it was a hotel, first and foremost. Did I dare ask if she wanted me to book us a room? I shrugged. *Why not?* What was the worst thing she could say? No? Not yet? I texted back.

Shall I book us a room there? We can have dinner. A spa appointment? Stay the night?

Make love until we're both exhausted and satisfied in a way we've never been before... I mused wistfully.

She didn't text back immediately,

So, I waited. And waited. I went and brushed my teeth, used the toilet, and checked my phone again.

Finally, she sent back a message.

Yes, please.

I punched the air in triumph, which was absolutely juvenile, but I thought whooping for joy aloud would probably draw more attention from Chastity than was desirable at this point in time

Will do. Meet you there at seven PM?

She replied promptly.

See you then.

I fell onto the bed, my heart thumping hard in my chest. It hadn't been that long since I'd had a woman in my bed. But it had been years since I'd bedded someone I cared deeply for, and even longer since I'd had sex with someone I loved—namely, *my* Kaiti.

When we'd dated in college, she'd been fun, dramatic, and intense. The sex had been amazing. A combination of explosive chemistry and an attitude ruled by the catch phrase "why not?" had set our nights alight. I'd wanted those nights to last forever. But once she'd fallen pregnant and suffered horrendous morning sickness, things had changed between us. Our dynamic wasn't the same.

Then after she gave birth, Kaiti changed. She wasn't my happy, go-lucky, free to love girl anymore. It got so bad, I wondered if she'd ever come back, and if she did, I never saw it. Our relationship ended in heartbreak and divorce.

Was that Kaiti still inside the Katherine I knew now? Tomorrow I'd find out.

I woke up excited for my night, but first I had to deal with Chastity. I suggested we go out for breakfast, it being Saturday, and that's when I learned her news. "What are your plans for today?" I asked casually over Eggs Benedict at a local diner.

"Well, Axel's coming over soon to pick me up," she said, not looking at me.

I froze, then forced myself to swallow the lump in my throat. "Oh, yeah. That's right. He's taking you out for dinner, isn't he?"

She nodded. "Yep."

"And what time's he coming to get you?" I asked, assuming he was coming to her, rather than expect her to go to him.

"About noon."

I glanced at my phone. It was already eleven AM. *Where does the time go?* "Shit. That's soon."

"Yeah."

I began to eat faster. My time with my daughter was quickly winding down.

"We've still got an hour," she said. "And I can tell him to come later, if you want? We don't have to rush."

"No. No… it's fine," I assured her around a mouthful. "Where's he meeting you?"

"He's coming to the apartment to pick me up. He thought he should come say 'hello'."

I froze with my eggs halfway to my mouth. *Uh… he what?*

"Is that okay?" she asked when I didn't say anything else.

I set my fork down and straightened up in my chair. This situation had just changed gears and I wanted to know what I was walking into here. "Okay, honey. You need to be straight with me. How serious are the two of you?"

"Are you really sure you want to talk about this?" she asked, biting her lip.

Not really, but I had no choice. "Yes. I think I have to know, or this isn't going to work."

She folded her hands in her lap and stared at me evenly. "We're serious, Dad."

That's what Axel had said too, but he'd been drunk at the time, and lonely from the sound of it. That didn't mean that either of them actually understood the definition of *serious*.

I narrowed my gaze at her. "What sort of serious? You've only known each other for a couple of weeks."

"Well…" She licked her lips nervously. "He's taking me to Vegas for my birthday next weekend. He bought me a car and purchased an apartment around the corner from my school."

I drummed my fingers along the tabletop in thought. That still didn't sound very serious to me. "Vegas is cool. I'm sure you'll have a great time. But none of that is unusual for Axel. He throws his money around to impress girls all the time. He always has."

And nothing she'd said, or he'd said so far, had convinced me that he'd changed.

She looked up again and sighed. "Dad, can you just trust me when I say that we're serious? We have no intention of breaking up."

I could trust her, but… "Has Axel told you as much?" I pried.

She nodded but didn't say anything else. From the look in her eyes, there was more to say, but there was only so much I wanted to know about what had happened between them, so perhaps it was a good thing she kept quiet.

Finally, I sighed, too. "Okay... I'm going to take your word for it. But I want to tell you one more time that I don't think he's the relationship type, sweetheart. He's just too old to learn new tricks." He'd never even been in a serious relationship as far as I knew. A forty-two-year-old bachelor didn't become a marrying man overnight.

"So... what? Why are you telling me that? *Again*?" Chastity asked, anger coloring her tone.

"Because I don't want you to say in six months that I didn't warn you." I put down some cash onto the check.

Chastity sighed. "Consider myself warned, Dad."

I stood up and hoisted my jeans up. "All right, then. Let's go. You need to introduce me to your first boyfriend." I'd been dreading this day for twenty years, may as well get it over and done with. I just never expected to 'meet' my best friend.

Chastity jumped to her feet with a grin. "Brilliant, Dad. Let's go."

And so, we did. We went straight back to my apartment, and I had the pleasure of having to wait for my best friend to come by. Not to chat, have a drink, or go for a run. He was picking my daughter up to go stay at his place for the weekend.

Heaven help me.

CHAPTER 12

Patrick

I'd managed to do the dishes, shower, and get into my running gear before Axel arrived. He was late, which was a rarity for him.

"Hey, beautiful," I heard him greet Chastity by the front door.

I cringed and moved further away so I couldn't hear any more from them while they greeted each other. *Yuck. My baby girl and my best friend.* That was going to take some serious getting used to. I moved into the kitchen and stood in the furthest corner, pressed against the countertop. But from there, I could see the two of them together.

Axel tugged Chastity into him and wrapped his arm around her. Then he walked forward and held out his hand like he wanted me to shake it. "Hey, Pat. Happy New Year."

I stared at him, then his hand. I really didn't want to do this. *Grow the fuck up. This is happening.* I sucked in a breath and thrust out my arm. "Nice to meet you," I managed.

Axel grinned like he was at a football game and his favorite team was winning or something. "This is a bit fucked up, huh?" he asked, breaking the ice.

Relief poured through me. "Hell, yeah."

Axel looked to Chastity. "Do you mind if your dad and I have a quick chat?" he asked with a gentle smile.

"Yeah, of course. I didn't get to have a shower this morning before breakfast, so I might go and take a quick one now." She pecked Axel on the cheek, backed away, then turned and ran down the hallway, abuzz with the elation of youth and love.

I sighed and let all the anxiety go with that one exhalation. "Shit, man... my head is completely fucked up." I ran both hands through my hair. "Trying to talk to you like my friend, but having to treat you like the guy sleeping with my daughter? It's fucking weird." I needed fortification. "I think I need a drink."

Axel followed me to the kitchen and pulled out a stool to sit on. "Go for it. It's past noon."

I grabbed the bottle of whiskey from above the fridge and turned to my old friend. "Do you want one?" I offered.

"No, thanks. I've got to drive."

Good call. For you, maybe. I, however, do not need to drive. I splashed some whiskey into a tumbler and downed the lot in one gulp. The burn in my throat didn't do much to appease the cold feeling in my gut, so I poured myself another.

"Look, man," Axel said. "I promise you... neither of us wanted this. It wasn't planned."

I gripped my tumbler, hard, and stared straight at him, my lips pursed. "Then why, Axel? Seriously."

"Because she makes me happy, Pat. Like seriously, nothing else matters in the world when I'm with her happy. And I've never felt that way before, not just about anybody, but *ever*—in my life."

I listened, but couldn't bring myself to respond, I didn't know what to say. Every time I felt like I was finally on top of these emotions, I got smacked in the head by something else. Guilt. Anger. Rage. Worry. It all piled up, smothering me under its weight. I couldn't handle it.

Axel continued when I didn't say anything, "Look, I'm serious about this relationship; about taking care of Chastity. I'm already in talks to sell part of the company so I can back off on the hours I work."

My mouth dropped open. *No way*. Not Axel! Not in a billion years.

He was Mr. Workaholic of the Year. "Bullshit. You wouldn't do that," I scoffed, sipping at my whiskey.

He shrugged like it was no big deal. "I'm already doing it."

I couldn't believe it. Axel literally lived for his company. But if he was trying to tell me that he was ready to prioritize something other than work, then the grand gesture was working. I shook my head in sheer disbelief. "I never thought I'd see the day you'd settle down, Ax. I mean... fuck."

And I still couldn't see it. It seemed truly impossible. It was like a leopard changing its spots! Workaholics like Axel didn't just undo twenty years of hard work overnight. But the intention was there, so I had to respect that. In the very least, it was clear he was trying to do something, to be more for Chastity.

Axel laughed. "You can say that again. And I'm sure you never thought it would be with your daughter."

Fuck, no. "No..." I began slowly, thinking about all the years I'd known Axel. All the women he'd dated. And my baby girl. "I definitely never thought this is how it would be."

Axel stood up from his stool. "Could I grab a bottle of water?"

"Yeah. Sure." I turned and grabbed one out of the fridge and slid it over the counter. "You have to understand why I'm concerned, Axel. I mean, you don't do relationships. You never have. And Chastity is *so* young, and she's got so many plans. You've got to make sure you don't get in the way of any of it."

That was what Kaiti was most concerned about... the possibility of Axel taking away Chastity's right to choose the paths she wanted to walk in life. How she'd always wanted it to go.

"I won't," Axel declared. "I want to support her in whatever she chooses to do."

That sounded like he was ready to pay off her school debt and move her into a cushy apartment where she'd never need to work. That wasn't what Chastity wanted, and it wasn't what we wanted for her, either. We wanted her to follow her head as well as her heart. And that meant sticking to her dreams and her career goals. The things she'd worked so hard for and been so dedicated to. We didn't want to see her become a rich guy's young trophy wife!

"Yeah, but you're rich," I reminded him, crossing my arms over my chest.

He groaned. "And I can't even pretend I'm not, can I?"

"Nope. I'd say I know all your faults and your virtues. There's nothing to hide."

Axel and I had been friends for so long, I'd seen him go through practically everything. From mergers that hadn't gone his way, to the women who'd waltzed in and out of his life. I knew he was extremely determined and smart, and a good person all around. But I also knew he barely slept, was addicted to work and exercise, and there would be no room in his life for a girl with a heart as big as Chastity's.

Axel stared at me, and I could see the serious turn the conversation was about to take before he even spoke. "So, you know I work hard, and I haven't committed before. But I love her, Pat, and if she'd let me, I'd just take care of her for the rest of her life."

That wasn't what she wanted. She wanted to be a chiropractor. "But her education—" I began.

"I said, *if* she'd let me," Axel interrupted. "But she won't. She's independent and wants to make it on her own. And I respect that. I love her even more for it."

"Good!" I said with a note of defiance.

Axel sighed. "Look, bud. The only way I'm going to prove to you how serious I am about Chastity is with time. When I'm still around in three months, three years, thirty years."

"Thirty years?" I almost laughed. "You really expect to live that long, old man?"

"Hey!" he said with mock outrage. "You're older than me, bucko."

I couldn't help it, I laughed. "Okay, Axel. All right. Fine. I'm going to give you the benefit of the doubt. But if you break her heart, just know, I'll make sure a weight bar falls on you at the gym when you least expect it." And I knew guys that would jump at the chance to do it, too.

He grinned and nodded like I wasn't serious. "Deal."

Chastity suddenly popped back into the room. "You two okay out here or is an intervention necessary?"

"Yeah, we're fine, beautiful," Axel said and reached an arm out to her.

She ran straight to him, and the look of love in her eyes was almost unbearable to watch. She was smitten. "You ready to go then?" she asked. "I've packed my bag."

He nodded and turned back to me. "Thanks for the talk, Pat."

"Likewise," I said and showed them to the door.

I had to sit on the couch for a bit after they left, to gather my thoughts, and was glad no one was around to see it. This was big. Both of them were truly serious about attempting to make their unexpected romance work. Kaiti was going to go crazy with worry about Chastity and her future. And it was me who'd be the one trying to keep her calm along the way.

When I got to my feet again, I didn't feel too great. Probably because I'd been stupid and had whiskey on a half empty stomach. Shaking myself out of it, I went to the kitchen to make a green smoothie and get ready for a run. Today was special for Kaiti and me. It was very possibly the first step toward getting back into a full-time relationship, and I didn't want the ghost of Axel and Chastity chasing us through the day or night.

It was time to clear my head and prepare to seduce my first love back into bed.

The afternoon went by at a snail's pace, which meant, of course, that when it was time to go, I wasn't ready. I'd done too good a job of distracting myself and ended up running a few minutes late. When I arrived, dressed in a new shirt and slacks, Kaiti was already waiting for me in the beautifully appointed lobby of the hotel. She wore a long black dress and when she turned to look at me, the beauty of the woman I'd always loved practically punched me from across the room.

I didn't hesitate. Walking right up to her, I grabbed her by the waist and hauled her into my body, needing the feel of the woman I'd never stopped loving.

She gasped but didn't complain.

I lowered my head and kissed her. Her lips were warm, and her flavor flooded my nose and mouth, which only served to make me hungrier for her. When I lifted my head, her lipstick was smudged, and she had a flush of arousal highlighting her cheeks. "Hey," I said with a winning smile.

She blinked up at me, dazed. "Hey, yourself."

"I'm sorry I was late."

She mutely nodded in response.

I took her hand, wanting to adjust my trousers, since they were now rather uncomfortable against my hardening cock, but decided against it. "Let's check in, then get dinner," I told her.

"I might just run to the bathroom first, is that okay?" she asked, touching her lips.

"Of course. I'll check us in and meet you back here."

She nodded again and raced off.

I headed for the registration desk, paid for the room, got two key cards, and met her a moment later. She'd reapplied her lipstick and wiped any proof of our passionate kiss from her face. I immediately wanted to pull her into my arms and smear her lipstick all over again, but I restrained myself from branding her once more only because I was pretty sure she wouldn't appreciate it.

"Let's have some dinner," I whispered into her ear as I put my hand against the small of her back and guided her toward the restaurant. When we sat down, I couldn't help but stare at her. Everything about her was so graceful. The strength of her posture, the softness of her hair, the way she moved the bangles on her wrist. It was mesmerizing. I'd forgotten just how much I liked to look at her.

"How was your day?" she asked after a time.

I grinned, not wanting to tell her the whole truth because the last thing we needed tonight was to get into a heated discussion about the pros and cons of our daughter dating my best friend. "Well," I began, "I spent the whole afternoon fantasizing about what I was going to do to you tonight. So, I would say my day was... good."

Her eyes went wide, then she reached for her water, taking an awkward sip. "Patrick, I—"

"There's no pressure, Kaiti. If you just want to take a bath, drink wine, and talk, we can do that too." It would kill me, and my balls would be as blue as bloody sapphires, but hey, I'd do anything for her.

She stared at me, her eyes shimmering with a vulnerability that I hadn't seen in her...well, ever. "No, it's not that," she confided quietly. "I'm just, a little... well, actually I'm a lot older than I was when we first met, Patrick."

I almost laughed but restrained myself, instead offering her a reassuring smile. "So am I, Kaiti."

"But you're still hot!" she hissed across the table. "You've got muscles on top of muscles, and somehow you're even better looking that you were twenty years ago."

"While I'm flattered, Kaiti, I—"

"No," she said, shaking her head adamantly. "Please let me get this out."

I waited, because what else could I do?

"My body isn't like yours, Patrick. It's given birth, it's tired, and old, and—"

"Kaiti, you're beautiful," I said, cutting her off. "Even more beautiful than you were twenty years ago." And it was true. Gone was the awkward girl, and in her place was a voluptuous, confident, stunning woman.

She shook her head again. "And I haven't been with someone for so long, I can't even tell you."

"Kaiti..." *Where is this leading?* I wondered, my brows scrunching.

"I don't want to disappoint you," she whispered, and this time there were true tears in her eyes.

My heart broke and was rebuilt, all in the same moment. "Sweetheart, I..." I stopped talking. There was only one way to prove to her how desirable she was to me. I stood up and held my hand out. "Come with me."

"Where are we going?" she asked, placing her hand in mine and grabbing her bag.

"We're going to our suite right now, and I am going to devour you. There's only one way to prove that I find you more desirable now than I did when I was a stupid kid."

Her mouth dropped open.

I stared her straight in the eye. "How about we order room service and I show just you how much I want you? Now. In bed."

Her lip quivered.

I leaned in. "Or on the floor. On the sofa. In the shower. I don't care where I get to make love to you. I only care that you come screaming my name," I whispered into her ear.

She sobbed a little as she sagged toward me, gripping my shirt tightly with her fingers.

"Is that a yes?" I asked her, my cock stirring to life in my pants.

She only nodded, her eyes still wide and teary.

So, I took her hand and dragged her toward the elevators. People said that actions spoke louder than words, and Kaiti was about to find out firsthand exactly how much I needed and wanted her.

CHAPTER 13

Katherine/Kaiti

My belly was tight and trembling, but not from hunger. My appetite for food had vanished the moment Patrick held out his hand and asked me to come back to our suite with him. *How scandalous!* We'd left the restaurant after being seated without dinner to rush off to the bedroom for sex. I couldn't believe this was happening to me. It was like some sort of wild dream I'd made up.

Instead of pinching myself to make sure it was real, I gripped Patrick's arm tightly and rushed with him to the elevator.

Unluckily for us, there were several other people occupying the lift, otherwise I had the feeling that Patrick may not have waited until we even got to our room.

"Which floor are we on?" I asked him, pressing even closer into his warmth.

"Seven," he said, just as the doors dinged open. "This is us."

He put his arm around me and corralled me out of the elevator and into the hallway.

"Which room?" I asked, making conversation because the intense apprehensive silence surrounding us was killing me.

"Here," he said, stopping in front of room seven twenty-six. "It has a balcony and a spa bath. I thought you'd like that."

I nodded, overwhelmed by his thoughtfulness. I loved balconies because I'd always enjoyed a good view and never had one of my own. And a leisurely bubble bath was the ultimate luxury for me. As a busy, and tired single mother, I could count the number of times I'd managed to have a bath over the last twenty years. They didn't even take up the fingers of one hand.

Patrick opened the door with a swipe of his card, then tugged me inside.

The room was beautiful, and so much larger than I'd anticipated. There was a huge, king-sized bed in the middle of the suite, with a mountain of pillows that looked super inviting.

"Patrick, I…"

He stepped up to me and pressed a finger to my lips. "Katherine, do you want to make love with me?"

I nodded anxiously, excitement bubbling within me, before leaning forward so my lips caressed his finger.

He pulled back and untucked his shirt from his trousers and took my bag from me, tossing it across the room to a chair nearby. "Then that's all I need to hear." He kissed me suddenly, cupping my face with both hands and plundering my mouth like a dying man who'd found water just in time.

For a moment, I was startled by the ferocity of his passion. Then, my own arousal caught up and I began kissing him back. I opened my mouth and slid my tongue in to taste him, wanting to get closer, needing to feel his flesh against mine. He'd untucked his shirt already, so I slipped my hands around his waist and pulled him into me, his body all hard lines and hot flesh.

He groaned and moved his arms down my form so that his hands grabbed my ass and hauled me even harder against his aroused body.

I pulled back.

He immediately dropped his arms away, his chest rising and falling, panting hard.

I stared at him, waiting for me. He wanted to know that I still wanted him, and there was nothing more arousing than the sight of a man waiting for permission to ravage me. Especially this man. *My Patrick. My one true love.* I'd chosen to wear this particular dress tonight for a reason. It opened in the front with a hidden zipper which was cleverly concealed among the curves of the material.

I reached for the zipper and slowly pulled it down, feeling powerful yet completely vulnerable at the same time as I revealed my older, but just as eager body to him.

He didn't move. He only watched on with salacious need in his eyes.

I opened the dress then pushed it off my body, letting it slither its way over my hips and into a puddle of fabric on the floor. My heart thudded in my chest with anticipation as Patrick stared at me. I'd bought new underwear for the occasion and was wearing a matching set of black lacy panties and a push-up bra. The lingerie showed my body off to its best advantage, but I was still old. I was still me.

Patrick rushed me like a bull, lifting me up against his body at the same time as his lips crashed down on mine.

I wound my arms around his neck and kissed him back, moaning loudly.

His hands gripped my ass tightly as he carried me to the bed.

In the next instant the backs of my legs hit the mattress, then we were falling and rolling, and I was on my back, beneath him. Exactly where I wanted to be.

"Get naked. Please," I whispered against his lips, hating the feel of his expensive shirt and pants beneath my fingers. I wanted the heat of his body, the softness of his skin, bare against mine.

He jumped up and pulled his shirt over his head in the way only men did.

I stared, wide eyed and lips parted, unable to help myself. "Oh my God," I whispered. "You're... sensational, Patrick." And he was. He was fit and well cut, and so beautifully toned and muscled. I couldn't quite believe how much he'd transformed his body over the years. When we were younger and married, he'd had no time for luxuries like spending time at the gym.

He grinned as he undid his belt. "Look who's talking, Kaiti. You're so beautiful, you're making my heart ache."

He pushed his trousers and boxer briefs down his thighs and stood back up.

My mouth dropped open as I stared hopelessly.

He grinned at me. "Well, as you can see, you make a lot more ache than just my heart. So, are you going to get out of those pretty panties for me?"

I nodded in awe, barely able to pull my gaze away from his long, thick cock. *Was it always been that beautiful?*

"Kaiti?" he growled, his tone low. "Are you getting out of that expensive lingerie, or am I tearing it off you with my teeth?"

"Oh!" Inspired to action, I pushed the panties off my legs and arched my back to unclip my bra and tossed it off the bed and onto the floor. Now, I was laying naked before him, exposed, and as he stalked forward. With grim determination I had to push back the desire to cover myself up. *Maybe I should ask him to turn the lights off?* But this was Patrick. The only man who'd ever truly loved me. I couldn't do either of us the disservice of asking for darkness to hide in.

He kneeled down next to the bed and spread my thighs open.

I gasped and tucked my pelvis under, trying to pull away from his gaze. What was he thinking, looking at me *there* like that?

"Sweetheart, relax. I'm going to love you so much. You just have to lay back and enjoy it, okay?"

I nodded and covered my face with my hands in embarrassment. "Okay." I opened my legs for, though my stomach trembled with fear. I felt so self-conscious I thought I might be sick. But then Patrick set his hands on me, and I moaned at the heat in his skin against mine. The pleasure that even the smallest touch from him gave me was phenomenal.

Then he put his lips on me, first to the inside of my thigh, then on my belly, and around to the other side of me. With each kiss, he moved closer to the core of me.

Damn, I wanted him to kiss me there so much!

He finally circled back around to my clit.

I moved my hips, begging him to finally kiss me where I was aching to feel him.

"God, I've missed you," were the last words Patrick said before he pressed his lips to my clit and began to suckle and lick me.

"Oh my God!" I cried out, arching my back almost immediately and grabbing for his hair with one of my hands.

He didn't slow down. Instead, he moved his tongue faster, flicking my clit relentlessly.

I screamed with pleasure, thrashing my head from side to side. It felt so incredible it was almost unbearable!

Patrick moved his hand up and slid two fingers inside me.

I cried out again, the sensation exquisite after having gone so long without.

He used his fingers and tongue like a master, pushing me higher and faster along the road to my first orgasm of the night.

"Patrick, I... you need to stop. I'm—" I was going to come. But it was going to be too hard and too fast. I couldn't help it. I couldn't hold back.

But he didn't stop. In fact, his tongue danced faster, brutally pushing me closer and close to the edge.

I grabbed frantic fistfuls of the sheets with both hands, clinging to the bed for dear life. My release hit me like a wave on the open ocean. It crashed into me, stealing my breath away; starving me of oxygen, light, and sound. And then I was back, thrashing on the bed like a cut snake, clinging to Patrick as I shuddered under him.

Over and over, the ripples of wickedly pure sensation pulsed over me, turning me into a blithering mess. I trembled and shook in its impossible wake, gasping for air like a fish above water.

Then Patrick was moving up, and between my legs. "Move up," he whispered. "Put your head on the pillow."

I did as he asked, though moving with limbs that were weighed down by pleasure was a feat in itself. Finally, I made it, resting my head on the pillowcase, and I sighed, bliss stealing over me. *It's been too long.*

"Don't go to sleep just yet," Patrick scolded sexily, lifting my leg so he could slide between my thighs. "We're not finished here yet."

I closed my eyes and languidly wound my arms around his neck, pulling him down for a kiss. Then I felt his cock nudge my entrance; the door to the part of me that had been empty for so long. I opened for him instinctively, tilting my pelvis in invitation.

He groaned loudly as he thrust inside me, parting my wet lips and piercing my puffy flesh.

I gasped out aloud at the strange feeling. It felt so foreign, but so good. Opening my eyes, I stared up at him, then stroked my fingers along his cheek, simply staring up at his beautiful face. "I've missed you so much," I breathed, my heart in my throat.

He drove into me, hard and fast, tearing a strained moan from me, and a mirrored groan from his own chest. He stayed that way for a moment, deep inside me, collecting himself.

I wrapped my legs around his waist, urging him deeper. I wanted more. I wanted it all.

"Kaiti," Patrick whispered.

With unmatched passion I kissed him, loving our connection on every level. I felt exposed, but full. Open but loved. *This is what I've been missing out on.*

He kissed me hard, pulled back, then drove into me again.

I allowed him to break the kiss only so I could get closer. I sank my teeth into his shoulder as he began to ride me harder and faster, pumping and pushing us both toward that final frontier, that ultimate peak—together.

I scratched his back, raking my nails across his flesh as I bucked my hips, meeting him thrust for thrust.

He fucked me hard, with more zest and power than he ever had. The headboard thumped into the wall behind us.

But I didn't care. I urged him on. *More. Harder. Faster.*

We rode the storm together, my body clinging tightly to his, getting tighter, and more twisted inside.

I was going to come again! I could feel the tingles of pleasure starting to course down the backs of my thighs.

Then Patrick began to groan. His movements grew jerky, and he halted unexpectedly.

I cried out at the denial and grabbed his perfect ass, hauling him into me.

He buried his head in my neck, groaning loudly and shuddering violently over the top of me.

His orgasm triggered my own, and with each pulse of his heat within my body, my pussy milked his cock like a bitch starved. Over and over, the blinding, primal pleasure shot through me, rippling over my entire body until there was nothing left of me but a gasping, spent, and sated woman.

I collapsed beneath him, and he rolled to the side, still connected to me, I held my legs tightly around him still, unwilling to let him go.

He was smiling and sweat dotted his brow. Patrick looked magnificent. "Wow," he groaned, breathless.

I laughed, my belly trembling. I couldn't help it. *That's the understatement of the century!* "You're telling me," I breathed. "Wow is right."

We untangled ourselves and I snuggled into his chest, listening to the steady, thumping rhythm of his heart. It sounded so familiar, so right.

He kissed the top of my head and pulled the covers over us. "We should order some room service."

"Hm. In a minute," I said, closing my eyes. I never wanted to move again. No moment had ever been so perfect, which surely meant it would soon end. It was Murphy's Law, after all.

CHAPTER 14

Patrick

I struggled to catch my breath. My heart thundered in my chest, and everything inside of me felt electric. I was far too awake, like a live wire, to follow Kaiti into post-orgasmic sleep. So, instead, I kissed the top of her head, inhaling the scent of her hair and gathered her closer.

I closed my eyes and shook my head with a small smile. I'd underestimated just how important and amazing making love to Kaiti again would be. Being with her was like coming home after a long journey. I'd never experienced anything like it. My heart felt like it was going to burst. It was *too* full. Everything about this was too much and too soon.

And yet the very idea of stepping away from her and breaking this very new connection between us... was unthinkable. I wrapped my arms around her even more tightly. There was no way I was letting her go. *Not now. Not ever.* The thought surprised me, and I stopped. But then again, after two decades of searching for a relationship that was even remotely right for me and coming up short; was it really that surprising I wanted the one woman who ever made me feel whole?

I just lay there, enjoying the warmth and weight of her tucked in beside me while she slept, thinking about how our lives were about to change irrevocably.

After an hour or so, she stirred, moaning softly,before lifting her head to stare at me.

"Hey, beautiful," I said.

She seemed confused, like she couldn't remember where she was or why the hell she was staring at *me* of all people, then the light of comprehension dawned in her eyes.

"Oh... ah..." She moved away to settle her head on the pillow next to me, the covers drawn up to her neck.

I chuckled and rolled deeper onto my side, letting the blankets fall to my waist. "Please don't tell me you're going to be all bashful now?" After all, I could still taste her pussy on my lips. Not that I thought that was a good thing to tell her at this moment in time.

"No, I, uh—" She stopped and turned her head toward me. "I'm just processing it all."

"Are you okay?" I asked. "Do you want a shower? Or should I order that room service?"

She sat up against the headboard, dragging the covers along with her. "I think dinner would be great, thank you. And a shower... yeah. Good idea," she agreed.

I flicked the blankets back and got up myself. "Mind if I join you?"

She looked absolutely terrified by the prospect.

Shit! Where had my confident, gorgeous woman gone? I sat down on the bed again, still naked. "Kaiti, what's wrong? Why do I get the feeling you're regretting what happened between us tonight?"

"I don't," she reassured me, shaking her head. "I'm just a little over-whelmed, I think. This has just happened so fast. Do you mind if I have a quick shower by myself and then we can talk when I come back?"

I didn't really like the sound of that but denying her the space she needed to think was never a good idea. "Of course," I said, picking up the menu and handing it to her. "Let me know what you want, and I'll order it while you're in there. And take your time. There's no rush. We have all night."

She pointed to what she wanted, slipped out of bed, and all but ran to the bathroom.

I shook my head and picked up the phone to call for room service. I ordered the grilled chicken Kaiti had asked for, added in some tasty sides and salads, some decadent desserts, and a hearty steak for myself. I was totally pumped despite Kaiti's self-conscious turn, and ready for a feast, before round two! Hopefully there was more to be had tonight, but I'd know soon enough.

When the water turned off in the shower, I was tempted to go into the bathroom and talk to Kaiti there. Some of my best memories of us were in the bathroom. Some of our best sex was in the shower, some of our longest conversations were in the bath, and Kaiti had labored at home in the shower for hours the night she gave birth to Chastity. But I didn't go in. Our relationship just wasn't at that stage yet. She wanted her space right now, so I was going to give it to her.

I lay on the bed and waited for the door to open. When she finally emerged wearing a thick, fluffy bathrobe, I smiled at her. "You look cozy." And thankfully, she looked like she was staying the night. The last thing I wanted was for her to leave after what we'd just shared.

"I am. Thanks," she said, smiling.

"Feeling better?"

She nodded in response.

My gaze ran over her once more. Her hair was washed and pulled up now, and her face was free of makeup. She looked younger, and definitely more vulnerable. "Come sit. Talk to me." I held out my hand.

She came, sitting on the bed next to me, but averted her eyes. "Can you put some pants on, please?"

"Why?" I asked. It wasn't like she didn't know what I looked like naked. We were long past that.

Kaiti laughed. "Because I can't have a serious conversation when your cock's out like that, so could you..." She moved her hand around like she could magic me to do as she asked. "Put it away?"

I crossed my arms over my chest, mock outraged. "You're going to have to tell me the real reason why, because as far as I'm concerned, I'm not getting dressed again until we leave tomorrow."

"Because I can't think straight when you're naked! That's why," she said exasperated.

I wanted to laugh but tried my best not to. But it took some effort, and the grin that spread across my face gave my humor away. "Well, thank you for the compliment."

"Patrick!"

"Fine... fine." I grabbed for my pants and pulled them on. I wasn't getting fully dressed again. *No way.* "Better?" I asked.

She nodded, but her eyes roamed over my chest in a way that made me thankful for every dead lift and weight I'd hoisted over the years.

There was a knock on the door, and I went to investigate. It was room service, so I let them in and waited while they arranged our food on the small dining table, before leaving.

I waved at the banquet before us. "Not exactly silver dining, but..."

"It's perfect," Kaiti said, walking over in her bathrobe to sit at the table. "It all looks great." She picked up her fork.

I sat down opposite her and grabbed my own utensils. "Don't wait on my account, beautiful. Dig in."

And so we ate, the only noises in the room were our appreciative moans and the sound of sipping and chewing.

When Kaiti had eaten her chicken and baked potato as well as some of the garlic bread I knew she'd like, she tilted her head at me.

"What?" I asked, raising a brow.

"I wasn't going to do this..."

"Then don't," I suggested. It was as simple as that.

She rolled her eyes. "Can we talk about Chastity, just five minutes?"

I picked up my glass of red wine and nodded. "Sure, she's our girl, but just until the end of the meal. Then it's back to us."

She leaned forward, her eyes gleaming with mischief. "What was with the car?" she enquired. "Did you see what he got her?"

I laughed. This conversation had just taken an unexpected turn. "A Beetle."

"Not just a Beetle," Kaiti said. "But a brand-new Beetle!"

I lifted my eyebrows at her in question. "You sound jealous. What's up?"

She sat back in her chair. "Well, maybe I am. I've never had a new car before. It's taken me twenty years just to pay off my tiny house." She sighed heavily. "I just thought I taught Chastity better than that."

I laughed at her in disbelief. "Hon, are you seriously try to tell me that you would have refused a brand-new car when you were twenty-two? One that was gifted to you?"

"But there are strings attached to it!" she exclaimed. "Is it in her name? Or will Axel just take it back when they break up?"

I shrugged. "No idea. But he's not that sort of guy."

"What sort of guy?" she pressed.

"The sort to take back the car if they broke up. There'd be no loan attached, he would have just bought it outright." Something I would have been able to do for her if she'd asked, but Kaiti and I had decided years ago that there were certain things that you had to earn. I leaned forward in my seat, feeling like a gossiping teenager and loving it. "You know he bought an apartment around the corner from her school so he could visit her?"

Kaiti gasped. "No way!"

"Yes, way," I said with a grin.

She frowned. "You don't think he… you know… bought that for her too?"

I shrugged. "No idea. Though it's entirely possible."

Kaiti threw her hands up in the air, quite literally. "For fuck's sake! Really?"

I laughed at her explosion and shook my head with a good-natured smile. "What's the real problem, here, Kaiti? You can't actually be jealous that our daughter has it easier than we did?"

"It's not that." She pouted. "You know what those rich kids at college were like."

"Yeah, I remember them well."

She crossed her arms over her chest, her ample cleavage in the robe exposed for my viewing pleasure. "They were bloody entitled, nasty, assholes. I wanted more for our daughter, Patrick. Working for your own things builds character. We spoiled her enough by supporting her through school so she barely had to work. But this?" She shook her head like all hope was lost.

I reached across the table and grabbed her hand, enclosing it in mine. "Sweetheart, a few extravagant gifts from Axel aren't going to ruin our daughter or undo years of love and positive reinforcement. She's alrady grown up. She has integrity. She's honest and hardworking…"

"But—"

"No buts," I said firmly. "And dinner's over, so no more talking about our daughter and her rich boyfriend. We should be grateful she's chosen someone who can take care of her, rather than some starving artist or something."

Kaiti grimaced in defeat. "I suppose you're right."

"Come on, sweetheart. Forget about Axel and let's talk about us."

"Us?" she repeated, meeting my gaze now.

I could see the stress of talking about Chastity and Axel just melt away. "Yes, us," I repeated. "I want us to be a thing, a real thing. Don't you?"

She licked her lips, her gaze furtive. "What would that mean?"

I laughed, then shrugged. "I don't know exactly. What do you want it to mean, Kaiti?"

She glanced down at the table, then met my gaze again. "Dates, dinners... exclusivity, at least until we find out if this is going to work or not."

I grinned, my heart thumping happily in my chest. "Fine by me. I'm the only man who is going to kiss those lips." *And I mean both sets.*

She blushed brightly, like she knew exactly what I was thinking. "And I want to be the only one kissing you. *All* of you." Then her eyes lit up. "Speaking of which. Can you stand up for me?"

I got to my feet, because how could I deny her? "Of course, but why?"

She walked over to the bed, grabbed a pillow, then dropped it at my feet. "Because you didn't let me touch you before. And I've been wanting to for *so* long." She dropped to her knees and kneeled on the pillow, then reached for the zipper on my pants.

"You really don't need to do that," I told her, staring down at her beautiful face. "This isn't a tit-for-tat scenario."

She grinned at me as she undid my fly slowly, which my cock reacted to instantly. "I know, but I want to," she said. "It's been so long since I've kissed him." She glanced up as my pants fell to the floor and my cock sprang up erect and hard to meet her. Her hand reached for and wrapped around the shaft, then she bent forward—her soft lips closing around my head—and took me to Heaven.

CHAPTER 15

Katherine/Kaiti

After our amazingly hot night together, Patrick took me out for breakfast, then we parted ways. Both of us had been grinning like silly loons, and part of me wanted to run away while everything was still perfect, so I didn't screw up and ruin it.

I knew I sabotaged relationships—I always had—especially since Patrick. Everything had been so fantastic with him... until I'd fallen pregnant. Then came the pressure from our parents, and the reality that I had to drop out of college. *The crushing of dreams*, I'd liked to call it.

Patrick and I had wanted to travel the world, to wait to get married then start a family. What should have been a joyous time ended up being a nightmare. My hormones were insane while I was pregnant. Totally off the charts. And my mood swings were nearly uncontrollable. I was like a walking, very round, ticking time bomb of anger and frustration.

Patrick had to find full time work to support us in a tiny apartment. He never had the opportunity to finish his degree, instead he was forced to work his way up the chain of command at a construction company.

I looked back on it now and could only see how I'd failed us both. I could have concentrated on my husband and praised him for all the work he did for us—on the sacrifices of his own he'd made. I could have

84

enjoyed my baby and our little home for the little snippet of heaven it was. I could have focused on making plans for the future.

Instead, I'd done nothing but spend far too much time lamenting the opportunities *I'd* lost. I blamed Patrick, my parents, and my own stupidity. It was wrong, I knew that now. Chastity truly was the best thing I ever did with my life. She'd given me more joy than any vacation, and more pride than any degree ever could have. But once I'd realized that it was too late. Patrick was gone, and life got difficult fast. *Really* difficult.

But now I had a second chance with him—my one true love—and I didn't want to blow it. Not again.

Sunday passed me by, and I caught up on all my normal chores, cleaning, doing laundry, and tidying up. I played music all day long and practically skipped around the house while doing it. I felt like some giddy, immature teenager, and I didn't care one iota. This was what happy was meant to feel like, and it had been so long since I last felt it, I was grabbing onto it with both hands.

Monday came, and I was back at work. Teaching was a rewarding job most of the time, and I was lucky to have a great group of students this year. Being in a good mood helped. Even the traffic during my regular commute didn't annoy me, nor the bitchy principal who always rode me about lesson plan deadlines.

When I finally got home, I made myself a light dinner and called Patrick, unable to stay away from him a moment longer.

"Hey, you!" he said, his voice warm and inviting. "I missed you today."

I curled up on the sofa with a grin on my face. "That's nice to hear," I admitted candidly. "I missed you too."

"Should I come over? Or is it too soon?"

I giggled and bit my lower lip, teasing it between my teeth. I was still a little sore from our night out, and my belly ached from all the orgasms he'd given me. "It's not too soon, but I do have a stack of papers to grade. Do you have work to do as well?"

"I do actually. Do you want to work together? I can bring my laptop."

"Oh, yes, please!" That sounded like a great way to spend the evening. I hated working through the night alone. It often drove me to drink a bottle of wine I wouldn't otherwise have.

"Perfect. Give me an hour, I'm just finishing up dinner. Should I pick up some dessert on my way over?"

I glanced over at my sad bowl of half-finished salad and sighed at his thoughtfulness. "That would be great."

An hour later, I was sitting at my small dining table surrounded by papers when he arrived. The doorbell rang and I jumped to my feet, my heart pounding. God, I was excited. I could barely believe how keyed-up I was! Smoothing down the black top I wore self-consciously, I walked to the door to open it for him.

He was standing on the stoop, looking way too sexy, his dark hair falling over his eyes. "Hi," he said, holding up a small paper bag. "Chocolate mousse for two?"

"Yes!" I stepped back to let him in.

As he stepped by me, he slid his hand around my waist and pressed a kiss to my lips. "I missed you, Kaiti."

I tugged him inside, so my neighbors wouldn't see me kissing my ex-husband, then pushed him against the wall next to the front door. "I missed you too." This time, I kissed him, sliding my tongue in to taste his familiar flavor. I wanted to be closer, but I could sense him pulling back, so I stepped back and indicated he should come in with a flourish of my hand. "Welcome," I said. "Come in." My cheeks burning with heat as I walked to the kitchen, my stomach tight and needy.

He came up behind me, wrapping his arms around my waist and kissing my neck. "Thank you for that delicious welcome."

"You seemed surprised," I managed to say, not wanting to start a fight.

He chuckled in my ear. "Absolutely. But it was the best type of surprise. Please don't take that as me rejecting you. Quite the opposite. I'm desperately trying not to fuck this up."

Emotion flooded through me, and I twisted around, wrapping my arms around his neck. "I feel exactly the same way. I know it was my fault that we broke up last time, and I don't want my bad moods and quick temper to ruin everything again." It felt good saying it out loud—taking responsibility—for the first time. Hopefully, if Patrick and I could avoid the mistakes of the past, we could move forward unhindered.

Patrick's eyebrows lowered, and he tilted his head to the side. "It wasn't your fault, Kaiti," he said gently.

"It was," I pressed. "I let my own anger and insecurities ruin what could have been an amazing time in our lives, and I just—"

"No. Stop," he said, then kissed the tip of our nose. "We were both young. We both made a lot of mistakes, and if we want to blame anyone, it should be bloody Rochelle. From what you've told me, she was sowing the seeds of our destruction for months before we even broke up."

A hot tear escaped my eye and I blinked rapidly, forcing it away. "Yeah, she did."

"Well, we can't change the past, so let's just agree that we were too young to realize what we had was real and amazing and focus on the future from now on. That is, assuming you want a future with me?"

I wiped away the single tear, laughed, then entangled both of my arms back around his neck. "I do. I *so* do, Patrick." I couldn't really believe everything had happened so quickly between us recently, but it had. And my love for Patrick had always been there. It'd never really gone anywhere, but for a long time, it had been buried under a whole lot of hate, anger, and regret.

But I was pushing those unwanted and hurtful emotions away, now, and beneath it all glowed a love and respect for this man that had just been waiting for its moment to shine once more.

"So, should I take you straight to bed and seal this newfound future? Or do you need to get more work done?" Patrick asked, one brow cocked suggestively.

I laughed, because really, what sort of question was that? "I can do my work tomorrow," I told him, knowing I'd have to get up at five AM to finish what needed to be done, but so what? *There is no way I'm missing out on this gorgeous man!* I'd already wasted too much time.

He grinned and held up the bag of dessert. "So, this is going to be how it works. You get to eat one, and I get to eat the other one *off* you."

I nodded emphatically, agreeing with his deliciously devious idea, because again, how could I not? *Hot bodies and chocolate mousse? Yes please!*

Together, we raced to my bedroom.

I threw open the door, then I stopped and looked to him. "You know, I've never had a man in here before," I admitted as the realization hit me.

He stopped dead in his tracks and stared at me too. "Really?"

I grimaced. "Yeah. I guess I just always wanted this house to be for our family—Chastity and me."

"And now, that includes me?" Patrick asked, sliding his hand around my waist once more.

I smiled, feeling the weight of the moment upon me. Heavy, lingering, and important.

Patrick didn't move, obviously waiting for me; my final decision.

So I tugged on his hand and pulled him into my ultra-feminine bedroom. My bed frame was white, as were my chest of drawers, and both nightstands. But my feature wall was a dusky pink, and I had pillows, curtains, and blankets in different shades of complimentary pinks, too.

Patrick didn't even bat an eyelid; he just followed me in and began to unpack the mousse for me. "Here you go, beautiful. This one's yours." He handed me a gorgeous little glass tub of chocolate mousse and a silver spoon.

"Oh, fancy," I said, opening the little dessert and taking a scoop.

As soon as the chocolate confection hit my tongue, I was moaning. "Oh my God," I exclaimed. "This is amazing."

"Well then, let's get you out of these clothes so I can eat mine too."

I was a little nervous to reveal my old underwear to Patrick, but I hurried out of my shirt, jeans, and underthings before I could let my uncertainty get the better of me. I wasn't going to be the one responsible for robbing this moment of its spontaneous passion!

"God, you're delicious," Patrick said, cupping one of my breasts and ducking to suckle on one of my nipples.

I cried out at the pressure, familiar, yet totally foreign feelings pulsing through my system.

"Lie on the bed," he directed, pulling at his own clothes so at least I knew I wasn't going to be the only naked one in the room.

I slid onto my pink comforter, lying back on the pillows, making myself comfortable while still eating my dessert. I crunched into the white chocolate covered strawberry that decorated the top and sighed as the sweetness exploded across my tongue.

Patrick smoothed some cold mousse onto my knee.

"Argh! That's cold!" I protested.

Patrick only laughed and lay down on the bed between my spread legs. "It won't be cold for long, I promise." Then he proceeded to lick and eat his dessert from my knee and thigh, catching the sweet, milky dribbles with his tongue as they slid down my warm skin.

I giggled and cried out at the strange feelings which combined so seamlessly with pleasure.

He did the same thing to my other knee, then to each nipple. Every lick and pull of his mouth made me gasp and grab for him, but he didn't stop. He was enjoying his dessert his way.

By the time he was done, I was flushed with heat, my cheeks burning with arousal. I wanted to just grab him and pull him into me. "Patrick. Please."

He put his empty cup on the floor and came up to lie between my thighs again, his head hovering over my belly. "Please, what?" he teased.

"Make love to me," I whispered.

"I am," he said, grinning.

I opened my mouth to tell him that he wasn't, that he was only teasing me...

But he dropped his head and pressed his mousse-cooled lips to my hot pussy.

Screaming out at the immediate pleasure, I grabbed hold of his hair as he ate me. I didn't fight him this time, or worry about my body, I just gave into his passion.

He licked and nibbled at me with enthusiasm, moaning loudly as he did so.

I cried out as my belly clenched tightly.

He crawled up between my thighs, ready to get into position.

Not this time, bucko! I pushed at him and rolled us, landing astride him.

His eyes gleamed with triumph, even though *I* was the one that had gotten what she wanted.

"You want my cock, Kaiti?" he breathed, his lower lip slack with lust.

I nodded, because that question was way too embarrassing for a woman of my age to answer. Dirty talk seemed like a young couple's game.

"Then take it," he growled, grabbing hold of my hips.

And those were the last words spoken.

I lifted myself up, slid up along his shaft, caught hold of the head of his cock, and moved back smoothly, engulfing him in one slick move.

A loud moan surrounded me. Was it Mine or his? I didn't know. But I had to move. The raw instinct to fuck was overwhelming.

Patrick grabbed tightly to my waist, guiding me.

While I pressed my hands down onto his chest, reveling in the feel of his hot, hard body beneath me. I raised myself up, then came back down, filling my hole and assuaging the deep ache inside. Pushing myself, I began to ride him faster; enjoying the way he pushed up with me, the swirl of our passion seething around us like a wild storm.

Then he moved his legs, planting his feet wide on the bed so he could thrust up harder and have more control.

My orgasm peaked with every plunge of his cock inside me, and I whimpered on the edge of ecstasy. Desperate for release, I let him take over, lights flashing before my eyes as the world fell silent. Grabbing hold of his muscular arms, I anchored myself as he cried out, his heat pulsing inside of me in erratic spurts.

Another round of orgasms tore through me, and I collapsed onto his chest, still shuddering, gasping for breath as a sob caught in my throat.

Patrick kissed the top of my head and stroked my hair, holding me tight.

How had I ever let anyone tear us apart?

CHAPTER 16

Patrick

Kaiti and I fell into a rhythm around work that meant we messaged each other when we could and caught up at night, if time permitted. We were both pretty independent and although I loved being with her again, it wasn't always possible to see her as much as I'd like. Especially with her wanting to keep our relationship under wraps for now.

The weekend finally rolled around, and I had the gym and a few meetings on Saturday, but we planned a dinner out on Saturday night concluding with a sleepover at my place.

After hearing how she'd never had anyone else in her room or her bed, I was determined to have the same atmosphere at my apartment. I called a bedding company, ordered a new king-sized bed and had it delivered on Saturday morning. My old bed went out the door, and with it, all the memories of the past twenty years.

Kaiti and I needed to start fresh, without ghosts haunting us or scars impeding us from moving forward. Was that even possible? I wasn't sure. But I certainly wanted to try.

At seven o'clock I got dressed and headed out the door, excited about what the night might bring.

Kaiti had asked me to meet her at our chosen restaurant because she was out with friends for the day, and they were going to drop her off on the way through. So, when I got to the restaurant, Kaiti was already there, looking spectacular in a black dress that stopped at her knees, and boasted a dropped neckline that drew my eye straight to her cleavage.

"Don't you look gorgeous," I said to her as I leaned in to kiss her in greeting. She turned her head a little, so I only caught her cheek.

"Thanks. You look gorgeous too."

I frowned at her as we made our way into the restaurant and sat down. "What was that?" I asked, unable to keep my intrusive thoughts quiet.

She picked up her menu and glanced down at it. "What was what?"

"You avoided kissing me. Did I forget to shave or something?" I ran my hand over my smooth chin and cheek. *Nope.* No problem there.

She shook her head discreetly. "No, it's just that since we're not telling anyone about us yet, I figured we shouldn't let people see us being intimate in public either."

Now it felt like a deliberate insult, which brought out sarcasm in me. "Do you want to stop meeting at restaurants then?" I asked. "We can just skip dinner and go straight to a shady hotel where no one will ever see us."

Kaiti rolled her eyes, not taking the bait, and continued to peruse the menu.

"Seriously?" I asked. "You want us to act like we barely know each other, instead of people who were married for years?"

"We're divorced," Kaiti said, flicking her gaze up and that's when I saw the hint of anger in her eyes. "I don't want anything to jeopardize the lives we've built."

"What lives?" I hissed at her. "What are you talking about?"

She put down the menu and looked straight at me. "Patrick, you have a job, an apartment, a social life that some of us could only dream of..."

"*What* are you talking about?" I ground out. "My job is boring me to tears, my apartment is tiny, and my social life...? I haven't even gone to the gym this week, so I don't know what you're talking about."

She glanced down and turned her head away. The curve of her throat and neck had always entranced me. So elegant and smooth. "I thought you went out a lot."

"I don't. Especially now that I'm not talking to my best friend anymore."

"What about Thursday night? Did you do anything special?" she asked.

Thursday night... Thursday night... "I had a late meeting, then did some grocery shopping. Nothing out of the ordinary." Then it dawned on me. She was fishing for something! "What's happened, Kaiti?"

"Oh, just a woman I work with said she saw you out at Maxine's on Thursday night with a woman. Apparently, she was young, blonde..."

My mouth dropped open. "Are you serious? Are we back to this again? You're going to actually believe some random woman from work over me? The man who has promised he wants a fresh start with you?"

Kaiti narrowed her eyes at me. "She isn't just some random woman. I've known Coral for over ten years."

"And has she ever met me?" I pressed.

Kaiti faltered. "Ah, well, no. But..."

"So, she's never met me, which means she only knows my face from a photo on your phone or from some with Chastity. And you really think there's no way she could have made a mistake? Confused me with some other the forty-year-old guy with brown hair?" I was getting angry now and finding it difficult to keep the bite out of my voice.

Kaiti's cheeks flushed red. "Ah... she might have."

"Yeah, I think she might have as well," I retorted. I was half a minute away from canceling dinner and going home.

Then our waiter arrived.

Kaiti called for his attention and ordered.

I held my tongue, deciding to see this date through, and ordered a steak, same as her. Simple meals so hopefully we could get out of here quicker.

When the waiter left, Kaiti attempted to fix her mistake. "I'm sorry if she was wrong."

I clenched my teeth together. That was a half-assed apology if ever

I'd heard one. "She wasn't wrong, *you* were wrong. Wrong to believe her without asking me. Then wrong for believing her over me when I told you the truth. If I had proof of where I'd been on Thursday night, I'd show you. But I'm sorry, I don't take selfies at the grocery store."

She looked down, feeling embarrassed or sorry for herself, I wasn't sure.

There was a heavy silence between us now, and I was in no mood to fill it. So, I left it.

Then her phone rang, and she looked at it quickly. "Oh, I'm so sorry. I have to get this. It's my mom."

My anger evaporated immediately. "Is she okay?"

"No... I'll explain in a minute. I'll be right back." She held her phone to her ear and raced to the foyer, which would offer her a quieter environment to converse.

I watched her, staring after her retreating form feeling a sense of DeJa'Vu. *Is this how life was going to be?* Was it destined to just be a repeat of our first marriage? Of questions and suspicions, and Kaiti avoiding the hard conversations.

When she finally came back, my stomach was twisted into a hard, angry knot. But I'd always liked her parents, so I had to ask to question burning on my tongue. "Is everything okay?"

She slid her phone back into her bag, "Mom's in the hospital."

"What? Since when? Chastity hasn't said anything."

Kaiti's lips twisted. "I haven't told her. I didn't want her to worry. She has too much on her plate already."

I raised an eyebrow at her. "And you don't?"

Our dinner arrived and we got to eating and drinking our wine. Conversation died.

And for the first time, I was starting to worry if we should really do this. Maybe we had rushed into everything like the fools we were? I put my knife and fork down. "Kaiti, I—"

"I'm sorry," she said, interrupting me. "I shouldn't have believed Coral about you going out with someone else. That was wrong."

"It was wrong," I agreed, though now that she was finally talking about it, the sting of anger was gone.

"I'm not excusing my behavior in any way, but I want to tell you *why* I was so quick to believe her when I shouldn't have."

I nodded and waited for her explanation, giving her the opportunity to talk.

"I'm... I..." Then she stopped and covered her face with her hands. "I'm so bad at this."

"You're not," I said. "You're trying to communicate, and that's all I've ever wanted; to work things through with you."

She finally dropped her hands down. "That was our problem before, wasn't it? I shut you out when you wanted to talk."

I nodded, feeling the familiar bite of regret. "Yeah, you did. You didn't want to have those tough conversations that we needed to have to sort stuff out." It was one of the main reasons our relationship hadn't worked the first time. "I'll always tell you the truth, Kaiti. Even if it's hard or it hurts, I'll tell you the truth. Always."

Tears glistened in her big, blue eyes. "Do you still love me, Patrick?"

The air left my lungs, but I'd promised her the truth, so I gave it to her. "I never stopped, sweetheart."

The tears slipped down her cheeks and she covered her mouth with her fingers as a sob emerged. "I'm so sorry. I don't want to mess this up. I really don't. I'm so stupid."

I shook my head. "Kaiti, you're not. You're just scared. I'm scared, too. I let you go once, and I don't ever want anything to come between us again. Especially not some stupid gossip. This is us. And this is *real*. And I'm in, if you are."

She nodded, and I knew it was time to leave.

I stood up and threw some money down on the check. "Let's go, sweetheart."

"Now?"

"Now."

She grabbed her bag and hopped to her feet.

I put my hand to the small of her back and guided her out of the restaurant and into the cold of the outside air.

"Where are we going in such a hurry?" she asked, seemingly a little taken aback.

When we got to a clear spot, I stopped, turned her around and dropped to my knee, right on the street.

"Patrick! What are you…"

It was too early to propose to her. We both had a lot of feelings and past issues to sort through first, but she wanted a big display of love, and it was time to show her how much I really wanted her. Not just for tonight, but for all of our tomorrows. I grabbed her hand. "Katherine Louise Shaw, will you be my full-time, totally committed, one hundred percent in girlfriend?"

She squeezed my hand. "Yes. Yes, please. I would love that."

I didn't get up, I had more to say. "No more jealousies or worries or insecurities. If I don't want to be with you anymore, I will tell you, do you understand?"

She nodded.

"I mean it," I added. "You will never have to spend a single minute worried about if I want you or where I am, because the moment we're not solid, I will tell you. We'll work through it, or we'll decide—together—that it's not going to last. Okay?"

She nodded again.

"Do I have your promise you'll give me the same courtesy?"

She laughed that time. "Oh, Patrick. You were my dream man when I was twenty-one and you're still my dream man. I don't want anyone else."

"Then you need to promise me that you'll stop sabotaging this, because I'm going to tell you to stop it if you do. I'm not twenty-one anymore. I'll damn well spank you if you need it."

This time when she laughed there was something else beneath the sound.

I got to my feet and pulled her into my arms, grabbing her ass like I owned it, which I kind of did. "Do you want a little spanking, Miss Kaiti?"

She slid her hands up my arms, no longer appearing to care that anyone could see us together.

"I've never tried anything like that," she admitted, her cheeks blushing pink. "So, I don't know."

Possibilities hit me and I grew hard. "Do you want to go back to my place and try a few things?"

She pursed her lips and nodded, all coy, and cuddled into me.

I grabbed her up, took her home, and showed her my new bed. She liked it more than even I dreamed she would, and by the end of the night, I had a mile long list of sex toys I needed to buy to try out on her.

We had our chance at a second chance, and I was going to share everything with her that we'd missed out on trying the first time around.

CHAPTER 17

Katherine/Kaiti

My weekend with Patrick was even hotter than I could have imagined. The fact that he practically proposed on the street had been incredible enough, but then to be taken home to a new bedroom suite, where no one else had ever slept, including Patrick... it felt like our wedding night all over again.

This time however, I wasn't pregnant or sick. Instead, I sucked him until he came all over me. Then he ate me until I came on his face. He spanked me and fucked me and gave me the sexiest weekend of my entire life. And to think that it was only the start of our second chance was just mind blowing!

He'd been right about me avoiding those hard conversations that could have saved our marriage all those years ago. I hadn't wanted to deal with the possibility that my husband wasn't happy with me anymore. Or the idea that he'd gone to another woman for comfort when I was at home with his daughter, depressed and not coping.

The conversation over dinner had been really difficult, but he couldn't have made me feel more secure or more loved. He was an honest man, and now that he'd sworn that he'd tell me if there was a problem with us, I had to trust him. No more listening to anyone else, or letting my fears run away with me. Patrick and I were giving it another solid try, and this time there would be no regrets if it didn't work out, because I was all in.

If I ended up with a broken heart again, so be it. But it wouldn't be for lack of trying. I'd learned a lot over the last twenty years and was hoping all those lessons would help me get it right this time.

On Tuesday, I got a call from Chastity on my way home from work. I answered the phone and put the call on loudspeaker and turned off the radio. "Hey, sweetie. How are you?"

"Good, Mom! How are you?"

I couldn't stop the smile that spread across my face at the real answer, but I wasn't sharing those details with my daughter. "Good. Work's busy, but fine. How was your birthday weekend?" I'd called her but her phone had gone to voicemail, so I assumed she was studying or busy with Axel—or both.

"It was amazing, Mom! Axel flew me to Vegas for the weekend."

My mouth dropped open. He what? For a second, I could barely breathe.

"Mom?" Chastity prompted.

"Yeah, sorry, hon. Just dealing with rush hour traffic on the way home. That's great to hear! Did you have a good time?"

"Yeah, I did. Vegas is amazing. Just like in the movies."

I wouldn't know. Our hardships, plus the divorce meant I'd never been anywhere. Not on my budget. "What was your favorite part?" I asked, trying to keep my voice light and happy though tendrils of envy were beginning to creep in. I knew it was wrong, so I kept the act up. No mother should ever be jealous of her daughter, but I was human too. I wanted nice things and to enjoy life... so, it was hard.

"Well, the food was awesome, and the atmosphere was cool. But I think I liked the roulette table the most. You would have been proud of me, Mom. I took out twenty dollars and played for hours."

Hot tears appeared in my eyes as I laughed with genuine mirth. She was still my smart and prudent daughter, even if she was sleeping with a billionaire. "I am proud, sweetheart! I bet Axel thought you were funny only spending that much."

"He thought I was crazy." Chastity chuckled. "He offered to give me some money to spend as part of my birthday present, but I didn't want any. Just being there was enough."

I finally pulled off the main road and into my street, parking outside my little house and turning the ignition off. "Finally, home." I sighed. "Are you coming back to the city anytime soon, sweetheart?"

"I'll try, but school is starting to ramp up. I've got two assignments due on Friday."

I smiled to myself. "I'm really proud of you, Chastity. You've done so well since your freshman year, working hard to make the Dean's List each semester." She'd done something Patrick and I had never accomplished.

"Thanks, Mom," she said, and there was a hint of something in her tone that I couldn't quite put my finger on.

"Are you okay, sweetie?" I asked.

"Yeah. I'm okay. It's just nice to talk to you."

I nodded to myself. Chastity and I hadn't been on very good terms the last few months. Her relationship with Axel had really caused some tension. But I had to be bigger than that and support her, because this could very well be a short-lived passion phase and I needed for her to be able to come home to me if she needed to.

"And how are things with Axel?" I forced myself to enquire. "Fine, I assume, since you had a nice mini break together?"

"We're really good, actually," she said. "Axel works a lot, but that kind of suits me since I'm so busy with classes and all."

"Hm," I said in a non-committal manner. Time would tell if she could handle the sort of workaholic tendencies that Patrick said Axel had. "That sounds perfect then, sweetheart."

"I've got to go, Mom. But talk to you again soon?"

"Definitely," I promised. "Bye." I hung up and glanced up at my house. My dark and empty house. Patrick was busy tonight, and I'd said that I was looking forward to a quiet night at home; some Netflix and a glass of wine... But as Chastity went on with her life, I realized that I'd been lonely for a long a time.

Chastity had been an easy-going, good teenager, then gone to away to college at eighteen. At forty I'd been an empty nester, while some of my friends were busy raising toddlers.

I sighed and carried my bags into the house, put everything away and took a shower. My breasts were strangely tender, and my body felt a little heavy. My mood today hadn't been great either, which usually meant one thing. My period was due. I checked my phone app just to be sure, and found I was spot on. I was due within a few days.

As I got re-dressed in warm, comfortable, tv-friendly clothes, I reminisced on how nice it would have been to be able to enjoy Chastity more when she was little. A lot of her childhood was a blur of barely managing to pay the bills, juggling multiple part-time jobs around caring for a child that never slept well, and my parents nagging at me for all the mistakes I'd made.

If I ever got to have another child, things would be very different. I'd work less. I'd be present more. And I'd enjoy every minute of the tears, the breastfeeding, the coloring books, and playing in the dirt. Just like with Patrick, I'd take what I learned from the mistakes of the past and try to get it right the next time.

But the dream of another child had been put to bed five years ago. At forty-three, I wasn't at an easy age for pregnancy or IVF. Some doctors wouldn't even consider using my eggs, and that was assuming we could harvest some. If I'd wanted another child seriously, I should have done something about it five years ago. But I hadn't and now I had to be content with the one beautiful daughter I had.

Opening the freezer door, I chose a microwave meal and while it cooked, poured myself a glass of wine. Before long, I had everything settled on the end table next to the couch. My phone rang just as I reached for the remote. I picked it up, happiness filling my heart. "Hey, Patrick. How was your day?" I asked.

"It was good. I worked late, went and had an early dinner at Mom and Dad's, and now on my way to Axel's."

"You're going to Axel's?" I repeated, confused. "Why?"

He chuckled. "Because I have to clear the air with him."

I frowned. "Did Chastity say something, or..."

"No. Neither of them contacted me, it's just—"

I took a sip of my wine and waited for him to continue. He sounded concerned. And I hadn't heard Patrick sound worried in a long time. "What's wrong?" I asked when he didn't immediately answer.

"I think I miss him. My friend. The guy I exercise with and watch football with. I know you don't like him, and for me he's definitely not who I would have picked for Chastity, but..."

I sighed. "You miss your friend. I get it."

"So, you're okay about me going and talking to him?"

I would have laughed, but from his tone, Patrick was actually worried about this and seeking my approval. "Hey, anything you need to do is fine by me."

"Really?"

"Really," I assured him. "Look, I don't like him, but I know you don't like Paisley either, so."

Patrick laughed out loud at that one.

I smiled in response, relaxing into the couch a little.

"Ah, yeah. That woman has more boobs than brains."

It was my turn to cackle. He was right. "So, you go and sort out whatever you need to sort out."

"I can't guarantee I'll sort anything out," Patrick admitted. "But I'm going to clear the air and see where the chips fall."

"That sounds like a plan," I said. "See you on the weekend still, yeah?"

"Yeah, of course. Saturday lunch at your place?"

I tugged the couch blanket closer and hugged it to my body. "See you then."

He hung up to take care of friendship.

I sighed, chewing on my lower lip as I picked up the remote. Patrick was definitely a better person than I was. I had no interest in becoming friends with the man sleeping with my daughter.

CHAPTER 18

Patrick

A xel had given me a key to his apartment a few years ago in a rather strange gesture that said louder than any words possibly could, that he trusted me. But as I held the keys in my hand, Axel's apartment key mocked me. I wasn't using it again unless one of them called me to say they'd literally broken a leg in the shower and couldn't get to the door to open it.

Other than that, we were back to being acquaintances, and that meant I knocked. I lifted my hand and rapped on the door; footsteps sounded on the other side as Axel headed over to answer it.

I was here to clear the air because I hadn't been sleeping well lately, and I knew it had something to do with losing my best friend. But could we work past what had happened? Honestly, I had no idea.

"Hey, Pat," he greeted, his tone and expression friendly.

"Hey," I replied, glancing into the apartment nervously and hoping to hell I hadn't walked in on anything lascivious this time.

"Didn't feel up to using your key this time?" Axel joked, raising an eyebrow in question.

I closed my eyes for a moment and huffed. "I'm never fucking using it again."

Axel laughed and held open the door wide. "I was just catching up on some work. Do you want to come in?"

That's what I'd come over for, though now that I was here, did I want to? *Not really.* "Yeah," I said, forcing myself. "If that's okay?"

"Of course," Axel answered and stepped back.

I walked past him and into the penthouse apartment, feeling as awkward as an ass.

"Do you want a drink?" Axel asked casually, though I knew he was trying his best to smooth things out.

I gestured to him. "Only if you're joining me."

Axel walked toward the fridge. "I suppose I could take a break from work for a while. It's been a rough day."

He looked like he'd had a bit of an off day, I noted. His normal calm, suave look was all messed up and he looked tired. "Oh, yeah? How come?"

Axel grabbed a couple of beers out of the fridge and popped their lids. "I hired a new manager, thinking he could take a load off me so I could get a bit more of a work/life balance, and all he did was fuck up some meetings and make things more difficult. Not exactly what I'd been looking for."

Hold on a red-hot minute. Axel wanted to decrease his workload? Since when? "You're doing what?" I asked, sure I must have misheard him. "Work/life balance? Who are you and what have you done with my friend?" Since when did Axel even know the expression 'work/life balance'? His work was his life. He'd purported to the fact himself, numerous times.

He laughed and handed me a beer. "Yeah, well, I'm getting old."

Now I knew something was wrong. *Old?*

Axel gestured for me to follow,

So, we wandered over to the living room and sat on opposite couches.

He groaned like he'd been standing for a week. "Shit... it's nice to sit down."

I almost laughed at him. This was a guy who ran ten miles a day with a shit-eating grin on his damn face. "You *are* getting old."

He took a swig of his beer and shrugged. "It's time to slow down. I don't want to keep working at the pace I have been. It'll kill me eventually."

That was true, but he'd known that last year too, and hadn't done anything about it. *So, what has changed?* I wondered. I gripped my beer and leaned forward. "What's the real reason, Axel?" Because if this was about my daughter, then I wanted to know.

He sighed and took a sip of his beer again. "Are you sure you want me to say it?"

I had to hear it. If Axel and I were going to be friends, I had to know what sort of future relationship we were going to have. As my best friend who'd dated my daughter for a month... or my future son-in-law. I swallowed hard. "Yeah. I've got to hear it, I'm afraid." I met Axel's gaze with my own, deadly serious about this.

Axel shifted in his seat and chewed on the moment for a minute, until finally he admitted it aloud. "It's Chastity. She's the difference, Pat. She deserves a good life, and I don't mean an easy life with money and diamonds everywhere. That's not what she wants."

I couldn't help the smile that lifted my lips. Kaiti was worried that Axel's wealth would spoil Chastity, but it just wasn't possible. She was already the woman she was. Money wasn't going to change her view of life. "But I'm sure you showered her in both all the same," I said, imagining just how much money someone like Axel would have thrown at a single weekend in Vegas. "Kaiti told me you took Chastity to Vegas for her birthday."

Which had actually been pretty thoughtful of him. Extravagant, but what a great place to take a twenty-two-year-old that had barely traveled. She would have loved it, and I wanted nothing if not my daughter's happiness.

"Yeah, I did," he said, then glanced away. "I bought her a diamond ring and got the most expensive suite in the place. But I think her favorite part of the trip was spending a total of twenty dollars over six hours in the casino. Seriously, you should have seen her."

I froze. Axel had done... what? Was he seriously admitting to having proposed to my daughter? Without even discussing it with me first? "Sorry. You bought her a what?" I asked, keeping my tone even while gripping my beer bottle as hard as I could without damaging my hands.

Axel's gaze flew to me then he shook his head. "Oh, it's not what you think! When I propose it'll be with your full consent. Don't worry, Pat."

That's good to know... but hang on a minute! I sat bolt upright as his words finally sunk in. "*When* you propose? Are you fucking kidding me, Axel?" He had to be. He really wanted to marry my daughter? Like... *seriously?* The perpetual bachelor wanted to settle down—for my daughter?

Axel leveled me with the seriousness of his face. "Yeah, I said 'when'. What's wrong with that?"

"But you're—"

"What? Forty-one? A hardened bachelor? A workaholic?"

"Yes!" I exploded. *Absolutely!* "All of the above!"

Axel slid to the edge of his chair and glared at me. "So what? What's that got to do with the fact that I love her and I'll make her happy? And just so we're on the same page, I'd honestly propose tomorrow if she'd say yes. But she won't because she wants to finish college first and you know what? I fucking *love* that about her. She's so fierce, smart, and loyal." He paused for a moment to glare even harder if that was possible. "I love her, okay? More than you obviously realize."

My mouth dropped open and I was at a complete loss for words, so I tilted my beer back and drank the whole damn thing. *Fuck... he is serious.* I knew that face, and that tone. He'd taken over a million-dollar company with less energy than he was putting into this conversation. He meant every last word that came out of his mouth.

I put the empty bottle of beer down on the coffee table and wiped my mouth with the back of my hand. I was stalling, but I needed a moment to figure out what I was going to say.

Finally, I sat back in my chair and took a deep breath. Technically he'd said similar things to me on New Year's Eve, but I hadn't really believed him. "Wow. I mean, I know you've said you love her and all that, but I thought you meant as a passing fancy to be honest. Someone to enjoy for a while, then you'd both move on when you'd had your fun. But you're talking—"

"Forever. Yeah, I am," he said sternly.

We sat in silence, Axel crossing his arms like an angry toddler and me just sitting, dumbfounded. How was I going to tell Kaiti all of this?

"Is that why you came over?" Axel demanded. "To learn my intentions? Because I was pretty sure I'd made it clear how I felt about her the last time we spoke."

He had... sort of. But... "Well, yeah. I mean, it's obvious from what Kaiti has said that you two are getting along, but I didn't think you actually saw a long-term future together." I didn't think Axel saw a long-term future with anyone really.

Axel narrowed his eyes at me. "Why not?"

Was he seriously asking me that? We'd known each other for ten years. I'd seen him go through more women than business deals. And he'd scored a *lot* of business deals.

I gestured to him. "Because, well... you're *you*, Axel. There's no way you'll find the time she needs around your work. And, yeah, she's at college for another four months, but what's going to happen when she moves away to study chiropractic? Surely, you're not going to do the long-distance thing. That never works out, not in real life." Surely Axel knew that? He was a seasoned businessman for fuck's sake!

Axel picked up his beer, took another sip, then set it down again. He was moving around like he was extremely nervous, which I could kind of understand. But he certainly wasn't the same cool customer I'd met a decade ago.

"Look, Pat, I want to make it work. I've been looking for the right woman for twenty years; so if it comes down to it, I'll sell the company, and move to wherever she is. None of this bullshit matters anymore." He gestured to the penthouse around him. "If I don't have her."

I took my time responding. He was serious. He'd give up everything he'd worked for, just for her. "She really means that much to you?" I asked, my heart in my throat.

"Yeah, she does. She means *everything*."

I stood up. I had a lot to think about. "Then I think I got what I needed."

Axel rose to his feet too.

I reached out to shake his hand. "Okay. Then I'll back off, and for what's it worth, you have my blessing." They were two consenting adults, and I had my own life to get back to. I wouldn't stand in the way of whatever joy they could have together.

"Thank you," he said, his voice so sincere it almost hurt to hear.

We walked toward the door, and I turned to leave.

Axel called out after me. "So, how are we going to do this?"

I twisted back around. "What's this?"

"Us. Pat, are we friends still? Or are you officially my girlfriend's dad, and nothing more?"

I inhaled deeply, then sighed. This was a conversation I'd avoided having with everyone, including myself. Mostly because I wasn't really sure how to do it all. Finally, I admitted the truth, lifting the weight from my chest. "I'd like to go back to being friends. I miss training with you. My fitness levels have dropped the past few weeks." Between work, and fitting in Kaiti wherever I could, I hadn't gone for a good run in ages.

Axel grinned. "I'd like that. So, what? We just talk football and work and shit?"

"Avoid personal talk?" I answered. "Sounds like a plan to me. See you, Axel" And I walked out the door. On the way down in the elevator I couldn't help but wonder what the future held for us all. I'd had so many surprises in the last month I couldn't even begin to imagine what might eventuate by the end of the year.

CHAPTER 19

Katherine/Kaiti

The weekend with Patrick was perfect. We talked about work and life. We worked side by side and slept spooned together. It finally felt like we were together, living our lives as a couple. It was scary, wonderful, and utterly natural all I once.

I still hadn't told anyone we were seeing each other again, because it felt like a dream. It also felt too new and too special to risk telling anyone about. I didn't want to hear anyone else's opinions on whether we were doing the right thing or not. My parents would have a very definite opinion on our reconciliation, and while I was extremely happy, at this point outside influences were not welcome.

On Tuesday, I realized my period was late, which wasn't super unusual, but a little odd. Generally speaking, I was pretty regular when it came to my cycle. So, by Wednesday, I was worried. My body showed all the classic signs of getting my period. I had sore boobs, and lower back pain; but still there was nothing.

Feeling a little jittery, I made an appointment to see my doctor. Pregnancy shouldn't be a possibility at my age. Not after only a few nights with Patrick. Surely? Perhaps I was I peri-menopausal? Or was there something wrong with my hormones? The last thing I needed were horrendous mood swings and hot flashes when I was re-igniting a rela-

109

tionship, but I was sure my doctor could sort something out for me. I knew there were medications that helped to balance you out when you reached that point.

I managed to get an early appointment on Saturday morning, and Dr. Lynda was extremely helpful. "It could be a number of things, Kaiti. We'll run some blood tests and take a urine sample, and a full work-up to see what's going on."

"Thank you," I said.

She was typing away on her laptop when she looked up at me as if stumbling upon an afterthought. "You're not seeing anyone, are you? There's no chance you could be pregnant?"

I tried not to look away, because there was nothing to be embarrassed about. "Well, I have started seeing someone actually. It's very new," I admitted.

Dr. Lynda reached into a drawer and pulled out a specimen cup kit, which surprised me. "Go to the bathroom, fill the cup at least to the line and snap the lid back on while I fill out the rest of the paperwork. Just leave it on the sink and a nurse will collect it. We can have lab results in minutes. There's no point going through a whole lot of other testing if it's unnecessary."

"But I'm forty-three," I protested.

She smiled at me for one of the first times during my appointment. The light in her eyes was a clear sign she found my statement funny. "I still think you should do the test."

I reached out and took it, my stomach twisting inside of me. "Okay..." I agreed reluctantly. "But I think it's a waste of time." It definitely was. I couldn't possibly be pregnant. But because the doctor had asked me to, I went to the bathroom, peed in the cup and left it where she'd told me to. Then I walked back to her exam room feeling foolish and strangely excited.

Do I even want to be pregnant? I wondered to myself. *No.* The first time had sucked. But the idea of another baby with Patrick... the chance to do it all right the second time? In many ways it would be a dream come true. So, when the results came back negative, I'd be devastated. Instead, I had to focus on the idea that I was probably just peri-menopausal, and I could look forward to fewer periods in the years to come.

The door opened and a nurse walked in, handed Dr. Lynda a sheet of paper, then walked out again.

I looked at her, my breath caught in my throat.

She stared down at the results, then handed the sheet of paper to me with a smile. "Congratulations, Katherine. You're pregnant. I'll still order some blood tests, but I'll change things to focus on your vitamin levels and check your overall health."

I blinked at her as I took the test results from her. "I'm sorry... what?" I breathed.

The doctor, who I'd known for ten years and was normally quite a serious, stoic woman, grinned at me. Actually grinned!

"Look at the test results. You're pregnant, Katherine."

I shook my head and stared at the piece of paper blankly. "Ah... I..."

"You're pregnant. About five weeks going by the dates of your last period."

My mouth dropped open, my mind whirling. "You can't be serious."

"I definitely am. Your HCG levels are strong. So, we'll book you in for a dating scan in a few weeks, but... congratulations."

My eyes welled up with tears and I had to swallow down the sob that rose.

"Are you okay?" the doctor asked gently, her expression soft. "I know this is unplanned, but I hope you can see something good in it?"

I buried my head in my hands for a moment, then came out of it laughing. "I can't believe it," I said, wiping the tears from my eyes. "I just can't believe it!"

"I'll recommend some good prenatal supplements, and we'll get you referred to an ob/gyn."

"Thank you," I said as I took my paperwork, still giggling at the absurdity of it all. I went home in a bit of a haze. It was too good to be true, which meant it probably was. Maybe the test was a false positive? Which I later Googled and found was almost impossible judging by my levels. The next thing I looked up were miscarriage rates in my age group, and by the time I'd finished exploring the Internet, I was thoroughly distraught.

When Patrick came over that night, I didn't know what to tell him. Any conversation he started, I ended up screwing up because I was only half listening. By the time we were ready for bed, he'd obviously had enough.

"Kaiti, seriously. You need to tell me what's wrong. You've been in your head all night. Remember, we promised each other last weekend to always be truthful with one another. And if something is the matter, we'll sort it out before it becomes a big thing we can't fix."

I changed into a silk nightgown I'd bought this week in preparation for a night with Patrick, so at least I was covered.

Patrick, however, was fully naked and way too gorgeous.

"I... ah... can we talk in bed?" I asked as I climbed under the covers and arranged the pillows, so I was sitting up against the headboard.

"Not exactly what I'd planned to do with our time in bed, but sure," Patrick muttered and climbed in as well.

The fact that he still loved me and found me attractive was bolstering, so I took a deep breath and started the conversation that had been swirling around in my head all day. "Did you ever want more kids?" I asked him, twisting around so I could see the truth of his expressions.

Patrick's eyebrows kicked up. "What's this about, Kaiti?"

"Just humor me, okay? Did you ever regret only having one child?"

"Regret it?" he repeated. "I wouldn't say I regretted it, but would I have enjoyed more kids if I could have? Of course. Chastity turned out great and now that she's off on her own adventures, it's hard not to miss her as a little kid, isn't it?"

I nodded. "Yeah. It gets pretty lonely around here."

"Yeah, it does at the apartment too," Patrick said, then he reached out for my hand. "I know we've only just gotten back together, but what do you think about us possibly trying out living together again? We wouldn't be so lonely," he offered.

I squeezed his hand with mine, a little surprised by the shift in conversation. "Really? How would we do that?"

"Well, I know you don't want to tell the world we're back together yet, but no one would even notice if we lived together full-time. I don't get visitors and neither do you, really. So, we could spend weeks at my apartment, maybe. It's closer to work for both of us. And weekends here, if you want."

I tilted my head, watching the emotions race across his face. "Is that what you want?"

"Of course, it is," Patrick said, pulling me closer. "I know we're both busy with work and just... life in general, but I'd much rather sleep next to you every night than go back to my apartment alone all the time. I miss you, Kaiti."

"I miss you too," I said and leaned forward to kiss him because he was too sweet for words.

When I pulled back, he had a beaming smile on his face. "So, would the week at my place work? Or do you want to split the time more evenly?"

I laughed and cupped his face, my heart overflowing with emotion. "I love you."

His expression became startlingly serious. "I love you too."

I tried to take a deep breath but struggled as the anxiety about what I was about to say next filled up my chest like a balloon. "Patrick, I—" *Oh my God.* Was he going to blame this one me? Would he think I'd done it to him twice? Fallen pregnant and trapped him all over again?

"Yes?"

"I... Oh, shit," I swore. "I don't know how to say this and I'm so afraid you're going to hate me, Patrick."

He frowned. "I could never hate you."

Well, I was pretty sure he'd spent many years hating me, but I wasn't getting into that conversation now. "But you could blame me, when I honestly had no idea that it was even possible."

This time he cupped my cheek and held my gaze. "What is it? You can tell me anything, Kaiti. I'm all in."

I desperately yearned to hide my face or change the subject. Everything in me was terrified of what was about to happen. But I had made a promise to talk things out and I was determined to keep it. I owed the love of my life that much. "Patrick, I'm pregnant," I whispered so quietly I barely heard the words myself.

Patrick narrowed his eyes at me. "Sorry... did you just say..."

I coughed to clear my throat and repeated the words with a tiny bit more courage. "I'm pregnant," I confirmed.

His eyes grew wide, and his mouth dropped open.

"And it's yours, of course," I added, though it was an unnecessary point, since it had literally been years since I'd slept with anyone else.

"Of course, it is!" he exclaimed. "I wasn't even thinking anything like that. I just can't believe it."

"I know," I agreed. "I couldn't believe it either. I mean, I'm forty-three. This wasn't supposed to happen. It wasn't in the plan." When Patrick didn't continue or say anything else, I pushed on into the silence. "And please don't think I did this on purpose to trap you or something. I didn't do that twenty years ago, and I certainly wouldn't do it now. That's not who I am."

Patrick stared at me, laughed suddenly, then grabbed my face and kissed me passionately.

My head was spinning, but I got the general gist. "Are you... happy?"

"Of course, I'm happy about it!" he said. "We can have a family again. With a child and a home. A *real* second chance."

Tears filled my eyes at the happiness I saw written on his face and heard in his voice. "I feel the same way," I whispered. "I wasn't sure how you'd feel, and I know it's way too early in our relationship for this, but—."

"Pah!" Patrick burst out, cutting me off with a smile. "I've known you for twenty-five years, Kaiti. It's not like we don't know each other well enough."

All of my tension and fears were beginning to drain away now, leaving an empty hole to fill with tentative, hopeful happiness. "That's true. But what will people think?" I asked, finally voicing some of my other concerns.

"What people, Kaiti?" he asked, his brows furrowed.

"My mom and dad. And Chastity! Oh, *God*, what's she going to think?"

CHAPTER 20

Patrick

I cupped Kaiti's gorgeous face with my hands and tugged her into me for a kiss. When she pulled back, I smiled at her and prepared to alleviate any and all of her stress. I wanted her to feel as happy about this development as me. "Chastity will be happy for you," I assured her. "She'll be happy for both of us."

"How do you know?" Kaiti asked, her big, brown eyes filling with tears.

"Well for one thing," I said, tucking some of her soft, dark hair behind her ear. "You already raised an amazing child, so everyone knows you're a good mom." That earned me a smile, so I continued, "And it was only a couple of weeks ago that Chastity asked me if I ever wanted to marry again and have more kids. Surely, that means she'll be happy for us and our second chance, too."

"I suppose so," she said, but didn't look entirely convinced.

Realizing physical contact would relax her, I lay down on my back and tugged her on top of me. "But do you know what?"

"What?" she whispered, nestling tighter into my chest.

I wrapped my arms around her. "I don't care what anyone else thinks." I kissed the top of her head and held her tightly in the circle of my arms, any notions of sex long forgotten. I'd wanted nothing more this afternoon but to come over to Kaiti's house and bury myself in her luscious body. But now I found all I wanted to do was hold her and thank God or whoever had orchestrated this miracle.

"And you're sure you're really happy about this?" she whispered once more. "You can tell me the truth. I'll understand if you're upset or shocked or whatever."

I ignored all her negativity and focused on her first question instead. "Happy?" I repeated. "Hell, no, I'm not happy. I'm fucking *ecstatic*. I can't believe how lucky we are, Kaiti. This is nothing short of a miracle."

She reached down and pulled the blankets up and over us.

Soon, I heard her little snores fill the room. She was fast asleep, but my mind was alive and far too wired to lose hours to sleep now. *I'm going to be a father again!* I crowed inside my mind. And not just a father, I was going to have another newborn baby, at forty-two; almost forty-three by the time the baby arrived.

I closed my eyes and searched my feelings. There was fear, doubt, and disbelief for sure, I was only human. But those emotions were in the minority, like singular clouds dotted against a bright and sun-filled sky. I had Kaiti back in my life and now we'd have another child together. How could life be so perfect?

∽

Well, as it turned out, it couldn't. A couple of weeks later, Kaiti was violently ill, which according to her friends, was a good sign of a healthy pregnancy; but to me, she looked like death warmed over.

"Are you sure this is normal?" I asked her as I handed her a bottle of water.

She was sitting on the tile floor in the bathroom, grey as the carpet outside the door. She took a sip of the water, growing paler, if that was possible. "I wasn't this sick with Chastity, so I don't know."

"When's that doctor's appointment, again?" I asked her.

"This afternoon at two PM."

"I'll meet you there, okay?" I didn't want to miss the chance to ask my own questions. This couldn't be healthy for Kaiti or the baby, no matter what her work friends said.

She nodded and gingerly got to her feet. "Yeah, you go. You're going to be late for work."

"What about you?" I asked, holding her hand and helping her back into the bedroom.

"I'm going to call in sick again. I can't work like this."

I agreed with her. There was no way she could teach in this condition. I went to the mirror and put on my tie, knowing she'd worry about where the money was coming from if she wasn't working. "What do you think about me moving in here full-time?" I asked. "I could sub-let or sell my apartment, then we'd have surplus money for when the baby comes."

Kaiti crawled over the mattress and lay down with her head on the pillow. "I don't know, Patrick. You love your apartment."

"No," I corrected her. "I love you. The apartment is just a space." And one where I'd had a parade of women I now wished to forget. "There's no rush, we can talk about it later. I just don't want you worrying about money if your sick leave runs out. I have money saved, and the apartment's paid off in full."

She closed her eyes with a small smile. "Thanks."

Despite her dismissal of the suggestion, I was happy to see that she didn't seem to be worried or focused on finances at the moment, at least. Stress wasn't good for her or the baby. I leaned over her and kissed her softly on the cheek. "I'll see you at the doctor's office. If you need me to come back and pick you up, just call me."

"I'll be all right," she whispered. "I'll see you then."

I didn't want to leave her, but hanging around and watching her didn't help either, I knew that. The past weekend she'd yelled at me for hovering, so I didn't want to suffocate her. It was a tough call when she was so unwell.

"Go," she said, not opening her eyes. "Or I'll throw a pot at your head."

I almost laughed as a memory surfaced through the worry. "I'd forgotten about that! You have good aim." During a fight after Chastity was born, she'd literally thrown a whole bloody soup pot at my head and given me a black eye.

"Go," she urged again, a little more strongly this time.

I finally, begrudgingly left because she'd asked me to and because I was getting more and more behind at work. Kaiti had been so sick the past week I'd often gone in late or left early. And today I was leaving at two PM for the appointment and probably wasn't going back in. I needed to catch up in a bad way.

I got to work and went at it like a madman all morning. At one thirty, without eating lunch, I clocked out and went straight to the appointment, where Kaiti was waiting for me in the sterile, white waiting room. "How are you doing?" I asked when I sat down.

She groaned but didn't answer the actual question.

"Katherine Kelley?" a nurse called out, stepping into the room.

I jumped to my feet and helped Kaiti to hers. Her hand was cold and clammy, and I held her tightly. "You sure you're okay?"

She nodded but again, didn't answer.

By the time we made it into the room, I was getting worried.

The nurse took her vitals and asked her some basic questions.

When the doctor eventually came into the room and looked at her chart, I was already pacing the room.

"Katherine, how are you?" Dr. Lynda asked, picking up a pen.

When Kaiti didn't immediately answer, I jumped in. "She's sick all the time. I'm really worried about her."

The doctor's gaze slid from me back to her patient. "How bad is it, Katherine?" she pressed.

"Bad," Kaiti whispered, a tear rolling down her cheek.

I reached out and squeezed her hand, my heart breaking at seeing how much Kaiti was trying to hold herself together, when she looked like she was mere moments away from totally falling apart.

"Feeling overwhelmed at this stage is very normal," the doctor said, pulling out the blood pressure cuff. "So, if you want to cry, just cry, and I'll see how the rest of you is doing."

Kaiti didn't make a sound, but tears rolled down her face as the doctor took her temperature, blood pressure, and asked her a few questions about her morning sickness.

"We have your initial blood test results back also. You're low in iron and vitamin D, so I'm going to recommend some supplements." The doctor wrote some notes down on a piece of paper and pushed it toward Kaiti.

She stood up to show us out,

I stayed seated and just stared at her. "Is that it? Seriously? She's this sick and you just want her to take some prescription vitamins?" I couldn't believe it.

The doctor turned to address me. "Unfortunately, there's not a lot we can do for morning sickness. Katherine needs to rest and stay hydrated, eat regularly and take all her vitamins. I can prescribe an anti-nausea drug, but you said you'd prefer not to take anything stronger?" The doctor looked back at Kaiti.

She shook her head and stood up. "No. No drugs. Not yet anyway."

I followed suit, amazed at the lack of empathy from the doctor.

"One more thing," Dr. Lynda said as we got to the door. "Your blood pressure was a little high today. If that persists, we'll need to monitor you more closely, but for the moment, just try and stay well."

"What about work?" Kaiti asked.

The doctor smiled gently. "Take off as much time as you need, but take it one week at a time. The hormones peak around week nine, so see how you do over the next few weeks."

Kaiti nodded but I could feel her stress levels rise from where I was standing.

"What if she can't keep down any water and ends up totally dehydrated?" I asked, refusing to open the door and leave.

"You take her to the hospital, and they'll put her on a drip," she answered.

Great! Last question. "Is this normal? This sort of sickness? She wasn't this bad with our first child, Chastity."

"Normal is subjective, but Katherine is doing really well at the moment. Hyperemesis gravidarum is the medical term for severe nausea and vomiting during pregnancy. The only treatments are rest, anti-nausea drugs, and hydration. If we need to admit her to hospital, we can, but there's no cure for this except to wait and see if the hormones settle down."

"If?" I repeated. "Did you just say *if*?"

The doctor nodded with an apologetic grimace. "Unfortunately, some women with GD are quite sick right up until they give birth. Others settle down in the second trimester. We can only wait and see."

"Oh, God," Kaiti said, putting a hand to her head.

I grabbed hold of her. "Let's get you home," I soothed.

"I've scheduled you for an ultrasound at eight weeks. Check at reception for the referral slip and I'll see you again in a couple of weeks. All right?"

Kaiti nodded and we left. She had taken an Uber to the appointment, so I could drive us home.

Anger and frustration coursed through me. I couldn't help my partner, and neither could the doctor supposedly. "We should get you a specialist," I suggested as we walked in the door to her house.

She nodded and slid onto the couch, laying her head on the pillow. "I think so too. Someone who specializes in older women, perhaps?"

I opened my mouth to discuss it more, but Kaiti had already closed her eyes and looked utterly exhausted. The appointment had obviously taken everything she had left in reserve out of her.

I went into the kitchen and got out some healthy snacks for her, then pulled out my laptop and started researching doctors. She needed more help, and I was bloody well going to get it for her.

CHAPTER 21

Katherine / Kaiti

Over the next few weeks, Patrick was nothing short of amazing. He set an appointment for me with an obstetrician who was brilliant. She was supportive, knowledgeable, and prescribed me some mild tablets that helped keep my nausea at bay enough to eat and drink. I'd gotten to the point where I couldn't even keep water down, so rather than be hospitalized, I took the medication.

When our eight-week sonogram rolled around, Patrick and I went in together.

"Why aren't you looking as excited as me?" Patrick asked as we sat in the sterile, white waiting room once more.

I squeezed his hand that I held and tried to swallow the lump of unease in my chest. "I'm just scared," I admitted.

"Scared of what?"

How did I tell Patrick about all the horrible things that could happen in a pregnancy? Especially in the first trimester? "What if the baby isn't healthy?" That wasn't my biggest concern of course, but I didn't want to tell him that I was actually worried that our little miracle wouldn't survive, period.

Patrick grinned at me. "How can it not be? He or she is sucking the health right out of you!"

I rolled my eyes but couldn't help the smile that tugged at my lips. He certainly had a point there. "I just—"

"Katherine Kelly?" the sonographer called out.

I jumped to my feet, my heart pounding now, and put my hand up.

The woman smiled at me, calling me forward. "This way, please."

We walked into a large exam room with an exam table, chairs and a lot of crazy looking medical equipment.

"You were told that today was a transvaginal sonogram, correct?"

I nodded. That's why I'd worn a skirt.

"A what?" Patrick asked.

"I'll leave the room for a moment so you can get ready, and there's a blanket here to drape over your knees." She smiled and left the room.

Patrick turned to me. "What's she talking about, Kaiti?"

I slid my underwear off and tucked them into my handbag. Then I hoisted my skirt around my waist and hopped up onto the examination table. "The only way to properly see the baby because it's so small, is to do the sonogram from the inside."

I could see he had more questions, but before he could ask, the sonographer stepped back into the room with a big grin on her face. "Ready to get started?"

"Yes, I am," I said, laying back.

She walked up and began preparing the equipment. "Is this your first?"

I shook my head. "No, our second."

"That's lovely," the sonographer said, applying lube to the large apparatus that looked oddly like my electric toothbrush, only bigger.

"Don't tell me that goes inside you?" Patrick asked, gaping at the probe, his brows almost reaching his hairline.

"Yep," I said.

The woman gently slid it inside me and pressed up into my belly.

I winced a little and forced myself to relax. It was definitely not the most comfortable thing in the world, but it wasn't as bad as I'd first expected if I was being honest.

"You're eight weeks?" the sonographer asked.

"A little over," I verified with bated breath.

"Ah, yes. There's the embryo, right there, and the heartbeat is visible too."

My stomach, which had been clenched tightly with worry, immediately relaxed.

"Would you look at that," Patrick whispered, a broad smile on his face.

I was looking, but I couldn't speak. My relief had turned into happiness, which had now translated to tears and a clogged throat. I wiped at the tears that escaped and leaked down my cheeks.

"Hey, are you okay?" Patrick asked, gripping my hand to reassure me.

I laughed through the utter maelstrom of emotion. "Yeah, I guess. I was just so worried."

"Let me just take some pictures for you, but going by the measurements, your baby's right on schedule. Eight weeks and three days. Perfect."

Perfect. That was exactly what I needed to hear.

The woman printed out our pictures for us and before long, we were back in the car on the way home.

"What are you hoping for?" Patrick asked, sounding excited. "Another girl or a boy?"

I pressed my palm into the flat of my belly where my tiny baby grew safely despite all my sickness. Seeing him or her there, alive and well, was still giving my heart jolts of happiness that rendered me speechless. "I don't really care," I said, shaking my head. "As long as the baby is healthy." Sliding my gaze sideways, I studied him as he drove the car. "What about you?" I hadn't really stopped to think if he'd have a preference or not.

"Me? I'd love either, to be honest. Chastity has been amazing to raise, but having a boy would mean we'd have both. So, no matter what, it'll be awin/win, really."

I relaxed back in the seat and smiled to myself. *Perfect answer.* "I'd like a little boy," I told him. "It would be nice to have one of each." Not that I'd have any idea how to raise a boy, but I figured that after raising a child by myself with very little help, this time would be a relative breeze by comparison. With Patrick by my side, I felt like I could do anything.

We drove home, ordered some takeout, and cuddled on the couch.

While we waited for the food, Patrick turned to me. "You look so much happier and more relaxed now."

I sighed, leaning forward to taste his perfect lips with a kiss. "I *am* happy and relaxed. It was such a relief to see the baby on the screen. It makes all of this so much more real."

"Our little smudge," Patrick joked affectionately.

I glared at him playfully as I pulled the images out of my bag. "Our baby is not just a smudge! There's a heart, and a head, body, and stumpy little arms and legs."

Patrick took the picture and stared down at it with a humorously crumpled expression. "Kind of looks like a frog."

"No, they don't," I denied, then looked again. *Yeah, they kind of do.* I shrugged the thought away. "It doesn't matter, as long as our baby comes out healthy in seven months' time."

The doorbell rang and Patrick hopped up to go and answer it.

I was still super sensitive to certain smells and food, but I'd found that if I stayed away from meat and ate regularly, I did okay.

"Your noodles, milady," Patrick said, handing me my rice noddle box before taking his chicken and beef to the other side of the room.

I smiled at him, love pulsing through me. He was so thoughtful. Always. "Thank you."

We dug into our dinner and while we were eating, the things I'd been worrying about recently surfaced once more. I had to ask Patrick what he thought, because he usually knew the best way to approach something. "Hey, what do you think about me telling Chastity?" I asked, forking some more noodles into my mouth. Those anti-nausea tablets were working well tonight, and I was able to enjoy my dinner without feeling too sick.

Patrick's head came up and he sucked a noodle into his mouth and licked his lips. "'I didn't think you wanted to tell anyone just yet."

"I didn't," I agreed. "But now that we've seen that the baby's healthy, well, I feel better about it, and think I need to tell her." Our secret had been weighing on me for weeks. Every time she called, I wanted to share our news. I'd always told Chastity everything. As she'd grown into a young woman, she'd become one of my best friends. Not telling her felt wrong on so many levels.

Patrick nodded slowly in understanding. "I will support whatever choice you make, sweetheart."

He got up and took his leftovers to the kitchen and brought back two glasses of water. "Do you think it's smart to tell her so early in the pregnancy, though?"

I put my noodles aside as my stomach twisted. Patrick was probably right. There were still weeks until I was safely into the Second Trimester. *Perhaps I should wait.* "Okay. I'll wait."

Patrick leaned down and kissed me, grinning like a loon. "What do you think about selling both of our homes and buying something bigger? A family house for our new baby and us?" He stood back up.

I stared at him, shocked. "You think we should... sell my home?"

Patrick frowned at me. "Well, both of our places are only two bedrooms, and I for one don't want to replace Chastity's things with the baby's. Surely, she'll still need her bedroom? I like the idea that she can always come back to us if she needs to."

I opened my mouth and shut it again. The baby would sleep in *our* room for many months after the birth. But then what? I wondered. "Can I have a little time to think about it?" I asked.

He nodded. "Of course. I'm just going to take a shower. Do you want to join me?"

I smiled. "Give me a minute. I'm just going to sit and make sure my food digests."

Patrick's eyes brows tweaked up. "What is it, sweetheart?"

I shook my head. "I can't put it into words. Can you give me a moment?"

He sighed, obviously a touch exasperated, and headed off to the shower, leaving me to my thoughts.

Everything in me was screaming that I couldn't sell my house. I'd spent twenty years scrimping and saving and sacrificing just to pay the mortgage each month. In fact, I'd only managed to pay it off a couple of months ago and now Patrick wanted me to sell it? I stood up and walked around the room, feeling angry and hurt when I knew I shouldn't be. But I couldn't stop the swirl of feelings. I marched into the bathroom where the water ran, and steam rose.

"Patrick, I can't sell my house. I'm sorry, but you can't make me."

He wiped his hand against the steamy glass door and peered through. "What are you talking about?"

"I'm talking about the fact that we've barely been back together for three months, and you want me to give up my house! A house I bought and paid off, by myself. Despite being a single mother, and—"

Patrick groaned loudly. "Kaiti, stop it. It wasn't my intention to start a fight, or to force you into anything. I just thought that considering we're having a baby and both own small homes, we could put our funds together and buy something bigger. Don't make me out to be the bad guy, here. It was just a suggestion."

I clenched my jaw, wanting to scream at him. I knew it was the hormones, and I was being completely irrational, but it didn't stop me from wanting to smack him in the face. The flood of hormone-fueled emotions was overwhelming.

"Just go for a walk or do something. That will calm your nerves," Patrick said, turning his back on me. "I'm not getting into this with you now."

I stormed off because he was right, and I hated him for it. *Damn hormones.*

CHAPTER 22

Katherine/Kaiti

By the end of the week, I came to the conclusion that I *had* to tell Chastity about the baby. She'd called twice during the week just to chat and everything out of my mouth was stilted and uncomfortable. I didn't know what to say to her, and I hated lying about what I was doing with my time. It felt dishonest.

I got up Saturday morning, took my anti-nausea tablets and had a cup of peppermint tea. Then I took off, my mind made up.

It was a two-hour drive to Chastity's school, so I took my time and got there before lunch. I parked the car, my heart hammering in my chest as I walked the familiar campus and found myself standing in front of Chastity's dorm room after following one of the residents in through the front door.

Okay, Kaiti, I coached myself. *Just breathe.* My knuckles rapped against her door before I had the chance to change my mind. I'd come this far for a reason, and I wasn't going home without sharing my news with my daughter.

"Come in," Chastity called out.

My stomach dropped. She was home. *That's a good thing.* I forced a smile to my face and some cheeriness into my voice and opened the door. "Hi, sweetie!"

"Mom!" Chastity cried, jumping to her feet and racing for me like she hadn't seen me in years.

I laughed happily as I hugged her tight. What a magnificent welcome. I couldn't have hoped for better. But soon enough I realized that something was wrong.

Chastity wasn't letting go.

I heard a sob echo in the room. "Hey, hey, hey. What's going on?" I asked, drawing back so I could stare down at Chastity, and brush the hair off her red face.

"I'm just so glad to see you," she sobbed, then pulled out of my arms to go in search of a tissue box.

Tears filled my own eyes. *Should I have visited sooner?* "Oh, sweetie. I'm so sorry it's been so long." I walked across the room and sat down on her bed. Then I reached for her and tugged her hand to encourage her to sit beside me. "Come. Sit."

Chastity blew her nose and mopped up her face with tissues. "What are you doing here?" she asked. "Not that I'm not glad to see you. I am, obviously, but I wasn't expecting you."

I froze, inhaling deeply through my nose. I wanted to be honest and tell her everything, and yet now that I was here and facing her, I was afraid. Insanely afraid. "I know you weren't expecting me, but I just woke up this morning and felt like I had to come and see you. So, I grabbed a takeout coffee, and here I am."

Chastity smiled. "Are you going to stay until tomorrow?" she asked. "We can go sleep at Axel's apartment tonight if you want. It's got three bedrooms."

She wanted me to sleep over? That was so sweet, but I had plans with Patrick. Now that I was feeling a little better, we had some *reacquainting* planned. "Um... thanks, sweetie, but I have a date tonight, actually. Dinner at eight. I can stay most of the day, but should try to head off around four, so I've got time to get ready."

She gaped at me. "Really, Mom? Wow! That's great."

'You think so?" I asked, hoping she meant that because I had a lot more news to share.

"Yes! Of course! You deserve to be happy," she said. "Who is it? Where'd you meet him?"

Oh, crap. I hadn't even told her *that* part yet! "Well, maybe I should take you to brunch and tell you," I said, jumping to my feet. Feeling a little nauseated, I needed to eat again. And hopefully, if we were around a crowd of people, Chastity's reaction wouldn't be too extreme.

Chastity frowned at me. "I just had breakfast, Mom. It's okay. You can tell me. Hope's gone for the weekend, so you can relax here."

I certainly could not. I began to pace the room. It felt like the proverbial walls were closing in on me.

"Why are you acting so strangely, Mom?"

Oh, God. I ran my hand through my hair. *If only you knew!* "I came all this way to tell you the truth, but now that I'm here, I'm terrified," I admitted.

Chastity stood up. "What is it, Mom? Quick, tell me before I think it's something terrible, or you're dating someone younger even than me or something!"

I almost laughed at that suggestion. Me with a twenty-year-old? *Ah... no. I don't think so. I'm not Axel!*

Chastity was looking really worried now.

I stopped my pacing and forced the truth from my lips. "It's your dad."

Chastity's eyebrows flickered and her mouth twisted like she's just sucked on a sour lemon. "Uh, come again?"

"It's Patrick. We went out for coffee a few months ago, just to, you know... talk about you, actually. And it was nice and comforting. We both had a good time. So, we had dinner, and another dinner. And then—"

Chastity pushed both hands out at me like a traffic controller. "Hang on a second. Let me get this straight. You're dating my father? After twenty years of being apart and completely distant, you two are together again?"

I nodded because I couldn't do anything else. I'd told the truth and had to deal with the consequences. "And there's something else." *Oh, God... please be okay with this.*

Chastity rushed over to me and grabbed my hands in hers in a surprising show of support. "What is it, Mom? Did you find him with someone else?"

I shook my head forcefully. "Oh, no, it's nothing like that."

"Tell me. It's okay. I'll help you if I can," she promised.

I laughed because she really was the best daughter I could possibly hope for. Tears filled my eyes, so I blinked quickly to force them away. "No, it's not like that. I just…" It was such a difficult thing to say. How did I even say the words? *I'm pregnant.* It seemed so simple and impossible at the same time!

Chastity groaned in impatience. "Go on, Mom, I'm dying here. So, you and Dad are dating again. That's good, right?"

I nodded and bit my lip, my heart in my throat.

Suddenly Chastity grinned at me. "You two aren't getting married again, are you? Because that would be kind of weird."

No, not yet. But it wasn't entirely off the table either. I tried to laugh but it came out strange. "No, it's not that. Oh my God, I wish it was that."

"Now you have to tell me. Spill!"

Chastity was still holding my hands, so I tugged them out of hers and walked away to get some breathing space. It was now or never. So, I put on my big girl panties, twisted around to look at her and spoke my truth. "I'm pregnant."

"You're… what?" she whispered, her eyes wide. "You can't be."

That's exactly what I thought! "I know, right?" I exclaimed, pressing my hands to my belly. "It's crazy, but I really am." I couldn't stop grinning now. It felt so freeing to finally tell her. The relief was almost a tangible thing.

"How far along are you?" she whispered, going pale with shock.

I certainly didn't blame her. "Only about nine weeks, but I had to tell you even though I know it's a little early to be getting my hopes up. I've been feeling *so* sick, but my doctor said my hormone levels are stable."

Chastity didn't speak.

I took a step closer to her. "Are you really upset?"

"Well, uh, I think I need to sit down," she answered. She then took a couple of unsteady steps before sitting down on her bed again. "Shit. Um—"

Once Chastity was stable, I began to pace again. "I know what you're thinking," I said, needing to fill the silence with all of my thoughts and feelings. "You're thinking I'm way too old to be doing this. I already had to give up drinking, which was not fun, I can tell you. And going back to the start, when I'd just finished raising you? It's crazy, I know. I'm crazy!"

But once I'd blurted all of my fears out, I rushed over to Chastity's side and sat down on the bed next to her. "But I've always wanted you to have a baby brother or sister."

"Oh, well—"

"And I know you won't be around the same way you would have been when you were little, but I hope you'd still want to be a part of this baby's life. Because I want them, Chastity, I really do. And your dad—"

Chastity grabbed my hand. "How does he feel about all this?"

"He's..." It was hard to describe just how amazing Patrick had been since the moment I'd told him. "He's really happy, actually. He's worried about me, naturally, but he can't wait. We both can't! This time will be different." It had to be. *I'd never survive losing Patrick again.*

Chastity was calm now and she started firing more questions at me as she processed the information. "What are you two going to do? Are you going to move in together?"

I bit my lip. Should I tell her that we'd been living together for a while already? "I think we will, probably," I hedged. I still hadn't wrapped my head around Patrick's suggestion that we sell our homes to buy a larger house. "We haven't decided how or where, but we've got a little time to sort it all out. Seven months, give or take." Which was surely more than enough time to decide what we were going to do.

Suddenly Chastity's eyes filled with tears, and she gulped loudly.

Guilt came crashing down on me. My daughter had so much on her plate with school and Axel and here I was adding to her stress. "Oh, no," I panicked. "You're really upset! I'm *so* sorry, my darling girl." I tugged her into my arms and held her.

She cried like her heart was broken. "I'm so sorry," she sobbed.

I refused to let her go. I just held her and rocked her like she was a baby once more. Hopefully all these tears weren't over my news, but if they were, I'd find a way to make it up to her.

When she finally sighed, stopped sobbing and pulled back, she reached for the tissue box again. "Don't go anywhere," Chastity managed to say, her voice cracking on the words. "I need to wash my face."

I watched my daughter go into her bathroom, my heart aching. Had I really caused so much pain? Patrick thought Chastity would be happy for us, but so far it seemed that she wasn't happy at all. Quite the opposite. She seemed genuinely devastated.

And it's all my fault.

CHAPTER 23

Katherine/Kaiti

When Chastity finally stepped back into the room, she was red-eyed and blotchy-faced. "I'm so sorry, Mom," she said straight away, moving to sit on her desk chair. "That wasn't about you. I have a lot going on at the moment, and I think your news was just the straw that broke the camel's back. So, thank you for letting me cry. I needed it."

Relief sailed through me. I had hoped that the crying hadn't all been about me and the baby. "So, you're not upset about my baby?" I asked her, wanting clarification. And once I got it, I'd find out what had gotten my daughter so wound up that she'd needed a decompression cry.

"No... not at all," she said, shaking her head. "I'm surprised, of course. But if you're happy, Mom, how can I be anything but happy for you?"

"Oh, thank you, sweetheart!" I jumped up to hug her again. Patrick had been right about her. *Completely.* She really did only care if we were happy or not!

Chastity put her hands out to stop me from advancing. "Wait, don't hug me just yet," she warned.

I stopped and slowly retracted, sitting down on her bed again, my brow furrowed. "Well, okay. How come?" If her pain and sadness had nothing to do with me. Then it was still something bad. Obviously.

Chastity grabbed another tissue as though to prepare herself. "Because I have news for you too, and you might not be happy with me, so let's try and save all the hugs for the end."

Oh, crap. This was about Axel. I just knew it. *What's he done now?* I took a breath to steady myself. "What's happened?"

She stood up and wandered over to the bed where a gorgeous bouquet of roses stood on display. "Well, I'm not even sure where to begin. Let's start with the shit news. Axel and I had a fight," she divulged.

Of course, they had. Long-distance relationships never worked, let alone ones with a twenty-year age gap and no common ground whatsoever. But I wasn't going to say, *'I told you so'.* There was no way. So instead, I calmly continued. "Have you two broken up?" Because it was only a matter of time, surely?

"No, I don't think so. He keeps messaging me to apologize, and he sent flowers, but I'm not ready to talk to him just yet."

I jumped straight to the first, and most obvious conclusion. A fight... roses for an apology... "What happened? Did he cheat on you?"

Chastity gaped at me. "Oh my God, no! Mom! Why would you think that?"

The fact that she'd even asked that question showed how little she truly knew about men. "Oh, sorry," I managed to mutter. "It's just Patrick has always said that Axel's been a player, and with you two doing the long-distance thing, I sort of assumed..." *And everyone else would have as well.* Why would Axel stay monogamous when Chastity was a hundred miles away?

She crossed her arms over her chest and glared at me. "You assumed that because you don't know him, Mom. He wouldn't cheat on me. He's got way more integrity than that."

I dropped my gaze because I couldn't even look at her while she spouted on about Axel's virtues. She barely knew the guy. Her hands caught my eye and I stared at the glittering piece of jewelry on her finger. "Is that the ring he got you?" I asked. She hadn't sent me a photo or anything, and now I could see why. That thing was expensive. *Very expensive.*

She stuck her arm out and wiggled her fingers like a new bride flashing her engagement ring. "Yeah, that's it."

I reached out and took her hand, then stared down at the antique looking ring curled around Chastity's ring finger. It was on her right hand, and wasn't a traditional engagement ring, but it certainly could pass as once. It was glorious, with intricately woven vines of rose gold, which entangled themselves around pink sapphires and brilliant white diamonds. Either I'd seriously underestimated Axel's feelings for my daughter, or he had more money than he knew what to do with. *Probably both.*

"He called it a promise ring," Chastity added.

Which was a traditional commitment ring from my parents' era. It was thoughtful and far too much for a girl of Chastity's age. But what could I say except... "It's beautiful, Chastity." I dropped her hand and slid back on the bed, so it was more comfortable to look up at her. "So, what happened?" I asked. How had they gone from mega-ring to a fight that required roses as an apology?

She sighed. "Basically, I wanted him to go with me somewhere important, he missed it because of work, and I'm mad at him for prioritizing his company over me."

Seriously? "That's a bit unfair, Chastity." The man had to work. It wasn't like he'd been out drinking or playing golf.

"You don't even know what he missed," she said, as though she hadn't deliberately been vague with the details.

"You didn't tell me, but from what you've said so far, Axel works his ass off, buys you expensive gifts and trips, and calls every night and would never cheat on you. All in all, he sounds like a perfect guy." And if he really was everything she said he was, getting into a serious fight didn't make sense.

"But—"

I could see her trying to justify her feelings, and I began to get angry. Chasity had never worked a full day in her life. We'd supported her in the hope she'd have an easier life than us. *A better life.* But with the full expectation that one day she would understand how difficult it was to pay the bills. "His success hasn't come from sitting around doing nothing all day, Chastity."

She rolled her eyes like a rebellious teenager. "I know that, Mom."

"Would you prefer him to be unemployed? Or a student like you?" Because if that's what she wanted, she should be dating a penniless artist. I was sure there were many of those right here on campus.

"Yes, I think I would prefer it if he was a student, actually," she retorted.

I stood up and glared at my smart-ass daughter. After everything she'd gone through to date him, then keep him! She'd hurt her father, and me, and now she was acting like it was a take-it-or-leave-it situation? "Then you need to break up with him, and go find yourself a nice, dumb, twenty-year-old. Because when you date someone twice your age, they have responsibilities you don't understand, Chastity." And I couldn't believe I was defending Axel, but I had to. My daughter had no idea what it was like to be an adult, and that was my fault. And Patrick's.

"That's a bit much, Mom."

Oh, really? "You've never paid your own bills, sweetheart. So please don't tell me you know what it's like in the real world, because quite frankly you don't."

Chastity deflated this time, staring at the ground. "Gee, thanks."

I took a breath and sighed loudly. How had we even gotten into this conversation? "Look, sweetie, you know I'm not a real Axel fan. I think he's too old for you. But I don't think being mad at him because he missed a date or whatever due to work is a good enough reason to break up. If he was playing golf or drinking with his friends, that's a different story."

She wiped her face, more tears now cascading down her cheeks. "No. He *was* working."

I shrugged. Then it was simple. "Then you're going to have to choose. Do you want Axel, with all his workaholic tendencies? And the money that comes with it, I might add. Rings like that don't grow on trees. Or do you want a guy your own age, who doesn't come with any of the money but with none of the responsibilities, either. Because people don't change, Chastity."

A wave of nausea passed over me and I put a hand to my belly and reached for the wall to steady myself. "Whoa, head rush," I explained. "I think I need something to eat."

"Hang on. I've got something." She rushed to her nightstand and grabbed some dry crackers and a bottle of water and handed them to me.

I immediately grabbed out a cracker and shoved one in my mouth and began to chew. "Thanks," I sighed. "You never made me this sick." I opened the bottle of water and took a grateful sip.

"So, do you think it might be a boy this time?" Chastity asked, changing the subject.

"I don't know," I said. "But if we want to, we can find out soon enough. Because of my 'advanced' age, they're giving me *every* test under the sun." It was called a *geriatric pregnancy*, which was outright insulting. But anything I needed to do to keep my baby healthy, I'd do.

"I can imagine," Chastity said, then glanced down at the ground.

Walking over to the bed, I set the bottle of water on her nightstand. Eating an actual meal soon was the best thing for me at this point. Maybe Chastity would be happy to go out now?

I opened my mouth to suggest we go and eat, when something caught my eye. Something black and white, and very familiar since I looked at my sonogram pictures every day. I scooped the photo up and stared down at it. This baby was more developed than mine. My eyes slid up to the corner of the picture where the date was printed. "Chastity, what's this?"

She froze, her eyes wide and scared, like a deer in the headlights. "Uh…"

"Chastity," I repeated, my voice unexpectedly harsh now. "Is this yours?" It had to be. If it was an innocent nothing, part of an assignment or something, she would have already explained. She wouldn't be looking at me with guilt and fear written all over her face.

Finally, she nodded.

My heart fell.

"Yes. It's from the sonogram I had on Wednesday, the one that Axel missed. That's *why* I'm still mad at him."

I groaned and threw the picture on the bed. *Fucking hell! No!* She wasn't supposed to repeat all my mistakes. I'd tried *so* hard to make sure it wouldn't happen. I pressed my palm to my head, where a headache was beginning to build. "Well, shit, Chastity. This wasn't supposed to happen!"

Chastity gasped at me.

I was far too angry to care. I *tsked* and shook my head. I didn't even know what to say. That sonogram made the fetus look about twelve weeks old, so she was past the point of no return now. There was no going back. An early termination wasn't on the cards.

Chastity tilted her head to the side. "Um... Hang on a minute, Mom. I don't think you're being very fair here."

"Fair?" I repeated. "You've known this guy, what? Four months? Five, maybe? And you haven't even graduated yet, let alone—" Then it hit me. *Oh, shit!* "Chiropractic school," I breathed. She couldn't go now, which meant her whole future was on hold, thanks to Axel. "You're going to have to defer. Oh, fucking hell, Chastity. This will really screw up your future if you go ahead with it!"

"Go ahead with it?" She gaped at me. "I'm more than twelve weeks along, and my baby is healthy. I'm healthy! Why the hell would I choose not to continue with it?" she demanded.

I put both of my hands on my hips. Didn't she know what she was giving up by doing this? Hadn't she learned anything from me at all? "Because it will ruin your future! Don't you see? You're just repeating my mistakes."

"Your mistakes?" She threw her hands up in the air. "Why am I always referred to as your mistake?"

Because getting pregnant at twenty-one *had* been a mistake, but it was one that had brought my greatest joy as well. However, that didn't mean that Chastity had to live her life the same way and follow the same path. *She could have it all!* Didn't she know that? She was going to miss out on so many things now. Just like me.

CHAPTER 24

Katherine/Kaiti

Chastity wasn't the mistake. *Not really.* She was a miracle, and an amazing child. But didn't she realize how much harder her life was going to be now? "I didn't mean it like that," I argued, trying to get her to understand.

"Oh, *yes* you did!" Chastity screamed at me, then stomped over to the other side of the room. "You always fall back on that excuse. Blaming me because you didn't finish college and have struggled with your life. But it wasn't my fault that you got pregnant so early!"

"I know that." It had been mine and Patrick's fault. One hundred percent. We'd been careless and paid the price for it.

"And it wasn't my fault that you made Dad drop out of school to take care of you or that you two broke up."

I crossed my arms over my chest. She was getting sharp now. *I would do a lot of things differently if I had my time again.* "I know that too. But—"

"But nothing, Mom," she snapped back. "This is different. I love Axel and he can take care of me financially, which is something you never had. I'll graduate from college even though I'll be twenty-five weeks pregnant, and if I never go on to the next level, then so be it. Axel said I never have to work again if I don't want to, and that's certainly not the life that you ever had."

I took a calming breath as anger began to build in my gut. She was looking forward to never working? That didn't sound like the daughter I raised at all. And if she was going to compare us, shouldn't she look at the fact that Patrick and I didn't even make it to her second birthday? Raising a child together was difficult.

"Chastity," I began, trying to order my thoughts and feelings properly. "You need to really think about this. A baby will tie you to Axel for the rest of your life. You don't know him well enough for that, and you're too young to realize what you're throwing away by having a baby this so early."

I'd hated having to talk to Patrick every week for so many years. Fighting about money, schooling, tuition, and bill money. It had been horrendous. And custody! *Oh, God, it had been a nightmare.*

Chastity didn't know about any of that, or how hard it had been for me. Yet she stood here before me, proclaiming that this man she'd known a few months was going to stand by her forever like some kind of knight in shining fucking armor.

"What are you talking about?" Chastity hollered again. "I know exactly what I'll be missing out on, because you've reminded me of it every day of my life. You didn't get to travel, graduate, or re-marry. Well, I'm not going to have any of those problems because Axel is *rich*. And he'll make sure we travel and enjoy the world. My life will be completely different from yours, and I can't believe you can't see it."

I threw my hands up in the air. I knew Axel had money! That was fucking obvious. But it didn't change the fact that Chastity wasn't ready for this. "You're the one that can't see it," I snapped back at her. "You're a baby yourself. You can't look after a child. You can't even cope with Axel missing one appointment because he was off making more money. You two will never make it and then you'll be stuck with a baby all by yourself."

I put both hands on my hips and glared at her. She was so quick to judge me and everything I'd gone through, and yet she was on the verge of making the exact same mistakes!

Chastity exploded. "You came here to tell me you have a completely unplanned pregnancy at the age of forty-three, with your ex-husband whom you've barely spoken to in twenty years, and you have the gall to tell me it'll never work?"

My mouth dropped open. She had no idea how much I loved Patrick, or how much I'd changed and learned about myself in the last few months. She couldn't judge me or our relationship on the past. We'd both grown a lot. "Chastity," I said, my tone telling her to back the hell off. She'd gone too far now.

"No," she said and stomped over to her door, flinging it open with theatrical flair. "You need to leave. But thank you for doing the one thing I needed you to do—put my relationship with Axel into perspective."

Oh, God, what have I done? I rushed over to my daughter and tried to grab her hands. I had to explain. I had to make her understand!

But she shook me off. "You need to leave."

"But—" I couldn't leave. We were in the *middle* of a massive argument.

"No buts. It's pretty obvious who needs a reality check around here, Mom. I have always supported you with whatever you needed to be happy. And today, when you needed me to support your life and your choices, I did. But you find out the exact same thing about me, that I'm pregnant to a man I love, and you fly off the handle and want me to get rid of my baby?"

Horror struck me square in the face. "That's not what I said!" I defended. I'd never have told her to terminate her pregnancy. But I needed her to really think about the consequences of her choice. It was my job as her mother!

"Well, you've said enough," Chastity snapped, sticking her nose in the air. "Thanks for nothing."

I took a step back into her room, I wasn't going anywhere. This wasn't how this conversation was going to end. We needed to sort things through. I opened my mouth to say something.

Chastity groaned loudly and theatrically. Then she said, "Fine. I'll leave then. Because I'm not hanging around here, waiting for you to go!" Chastity ran for her cell phone, then bolted out of the room, leaving me alone and stupefied.

I just stared after her retreating figure for too long, then stumbled over to her bed once more to take some slow, deep breaths. That had gone *so* much worse than I could have ever imagined. I felt sick to my very stomach, and my head pounded with the beginnings of a massive headache.

My blood pressure had been way too high lately, and I probably needed to just rest. But I couldn't stay here, not with Chastity fit to tear my head off again. I needed to go home, but first I picked up the sonogram picture of the perfect little baby Chastity was carrying. Tears prickled my eyes and my heart ached with the knowledge that unless I sorted things out with my daughter, this child and I may never know each other.

I hauled myself to my feet and managed to get to my car, where I sat and I cried, and wished to God I'd never driven here this day.

CHAPTER 25

Patrick

I'd gone into work for a few hours and had been waiting for Kaiti to call like she usually did. She'd been asleep when I left this morning, and I was beginning to worry about her. But then my phone rang, and it was my daughter. I picked up the phone and projected a smile into my voice. "Hey, Chastity! Long time, no talk," I said, scratching behind my ear.

"Hey, Dad! I need to talk to you for a minute. Do you think you can you spare the time?"

I got up from my office chair and walked along the long corridor toward the meeting room. "Uh, yeah, sure, sweetheart. Can you give me a minute? I'm just going to walk somewhere a little quieter." I glanced into the large meeting room nearest to me and noted it was empty, so I walked in, grabbed a bottle of water from the mini fridge and took a seat. "Okay, I'm good. Talk to me. What's up?"

"Uh, well, Mom visited me this morning and shared your good news with me," she began.

Oh, shit. A heads up would have been nice, Kaiti! Gritting my teeth, I braced myself for whatever was about to happen. "Oh, sweetheart. I didn't know she was going to see you, otherwise I would have come along too." My presence may have softened the blow a bit. *Maybe.*

Kaiti had been cranky as hell all week, so when she'd said last night that she had wanted to talk to Chastity, I'd been a little concerned about the both of them. But she hadn't told me she was actually intending on going today. I definitely wouldn't have let her go alone. She was a hormonal mess and a temper tantrum just waiting to happen. I sighed. *Fuck.*

"It's okay, Dad," Chastity assured me. "I know you try and do the right thing; you always have, that's why I'm calling you. I'm happy for you and Mom, honestly, I really am. You both deserve a second chance to be happy, and if this is it, then I couldn't be happier for the both of you."

I tilted my head back and closed my eyes for a moment, relief rushing through me, allowing me to ease up the tension in my jaw. That was exactly what I'd hoped she'd say. "Thanks, Chastity. I appreciate that. I've wanted to tell you for a while, but it seemed too early to say anything."

Kaiti was still in dangerous waters with her pregnancy, and despite the fact that we didn't talk about it aloud, I knew she was still worried about miscarrying. As a so-called *geriatric pregnancy*, it was forever in the back of her mind, stressing her out and putting her on edge.

"That's how I've been feeling lately, too," my daughter answered.

I frowned and shifted in my chair. "What do you mean?"

"I have news for you as well. I thought it was too early to say anything up until this week, then I chickened out on telling you when I had the opportunity. But Mom knows, now that she surprised me on campus, and she's angry at me. So, I wanted to tell you, myself, before you heard it second hand."

Oh, God... what's happened? And just like that the tension returned. Taking a deep breath, I sat straight. There was something in Chastity's tone of voice that was throwing me. "What is it?" I asked carefully. "Are you okay?" Had something happened between her and Axel? Is that why Kaiti was angry?

She laughed, though it seemed uncomfortably forced. "Um, no, not really, Dad. But that's just because Mom and I had a fight. But overall, yeah, I guess I'm good."

That wasn't unusual, Chastity and her mother fought like cat and dog from time to time; but if this was about us or our pregnancy, I needed to know. I couldn't have my girls at odds now, especially over the newest addition to our family—something which should be being celebrated! "Well, tell me, sweetheart," I urged her. "You're leaving me hanging here." I waited, ready for anything; like a soldier on the front line, prepared for whatever might come over the hill.

"I'm pregnant too," she said, knocking the breath out of me.

Oh, fuck. Anything but that. I crushed the water bottle in my hand as our parental worst nightmare was finally realized.

"Over twelve weeks," she went on. "I had my First Trimester scan on Wednesday, and everything is looking good so far. I've been wanting to tell you guys but didn't know how to say it because I knew you'd be disappointed in me. But I just wanted you to know that I'm still going to graduate, just like I intended, and Axel is going to take care of us. So you don't have to worry about anything, okay?"

That fucking bastard! He hadn't said anything! I squeezed my eyes shut and pinched the bridge of my nose, so that I wouldn't say something I'd live to regret. My daughter was pregnant at twenty-two, to a guy she'd known for all of three or four months? *Shit!* I reeled. I pressed my fist to my mouth to stop the groan of frustration that so desperately wanted to escape me. "Wow... I don't know what to say," I managed without gnawing off my own hand.

"You can ask me how I'm feeling, or what Axel thinks of it? Anything at all, really, Dad," Chastity offered, clearly seeking my acceptance.

But I wasn't sure I could give it right now. *If ever!* If I responded incorrectly or voiced something in a tone she didn't like, I'd be in the doghouse just like Kaiti was. Oh, God, Kaiti. *How's your blood pressure now?* I began to panic about her and the health of our little miracle. "I don't know what to say," I said again, because it was the truth. How did I go about telling my baby girl that she was right? I *was* disappointed, but mostly in Axel, my supposed best friend. *What an asshole move.*

"Okay, Dad. Bye, I guess."

No! "Chastity, wait—" And the line cut out.

She'd hung up on me.

I tried to call her back, to fix my fuck up, but it went directly to voicemail. I got up and began to pace the empty corporate room, my heart firmly lodged in my throat. I felt like the weight of the world suddenly just landed on my bloody shoulders and I didn't know if I was strong enough to bear it. "Oh, fuck." *What are we going to do now, Kaiti? What the fuck are we going to do?*

CHAPTER 26

Patrick

When I couldn't get in contact with Chastity, I called Kaiti. My heart was thumping in my chest like a drum of war building up to some great crescendo, making me sick to my stomach with worry. The phone rang out and went to voicemail, which *never* happened with Kaiti. Especially on a day I knew she wasn't at work. Fueled by adrenalin and no small amount of panic, I sent her a text.

Call me, please. I'm worried about you, Kaiti.

It was almost lunchtime, so I logged out, grabbed my wallet and headed out to the car. My day's work was done, it had to be. I couldn't focus or think of anything at all but getting to Kaiti as soon as possible. She had a two-hour drive ahead of her, and she wasn't even supposed to be driving! What if she had an accident? What if her blood pressure skyrocketed and damaged the baby somehow?

When she called me back five minutes later, I was already driving toward Chastity's school. "Hi, honey," she whispered.

"Where are you?" I demanded. "Are you okay? I'm coming to get you." I fired all the words at her like bullets from a gatling gun, not even waiting for her to answer.

"No! Don't. I'm fine," she objected, her voice hitching.

"You don't sound fine," I said, still driving. "You sound like you've been crying." She was all throaty and raspy, with that nasal quality that came with tears.

"I'm fine," she repeated. "Please don't drive all this way. I can do it."

I didn't think so. "It's not safe, Kaiti. What if you have an accident?"

Her breath shuddered out as though she were releasing a whole lot of stress. "But the car—" she argued feebly.

"Don't worry about the damn car!" I insisted. "We'll just park it somewhere safe, and I'll take Joe or Terry and go get it tomorrow or another day. The car is replaceable. You and our baby are *not*. Don't push me on this one, Kaiti."

There was a protracted silence, then a defeated and tired sigh. "What should I do for two hours?" she finally asked.

Relief and worry flowed through me. If she conceded that easily, then she didn't think it was safe to drive either, which was worrying in and of itself. "Talk to me," I said. "I'm already on the highway."

She sobbed a little, the sound painful and tragic.

My heart broke. "What happened, sweetheart?"

"She... Chastity..." she tried.

"She called me," I got in, so she didn't need to tell me anything I already knew.

"She what?" Kaiti asked, sounding clearer with her surprise.

"Yeah, she called ten minutes ago to tell me that she's pregnant and happy, and Axel's going to look after her." My grip on the steering wheel got tighter with every word, but I forced myself to keep my tone neutral. *Fucking bastard.* I seethed internally.

"What did you say to her?" Kaiti whispered.

I groaned aloud as traffic raced by me. "Nothing! I didn't know what to say, so she hung up on me."

Kaiti was silent at first. "That was probably what I should have done," she finally said,

A chill crept down my spine. Chastity had always kowtowed to her mother's personality, but they were *a lot* alike. Had the day come when Chastity had stood up to her? "What did you say?" I asked.

Kaiti sighed.

I heard a car door shut.

"You okay?" I asked cautiously.

"Yeah, I just need some fresh air. I'm feeling pretty sick right now."

I could only imagine. "What happened, Kaiti?"

"I—I got angry. I tried to tell her that she was going to miss out on so much. All the things she wants, like chiropractic school, travel, and the freedom and independence of her twenties! God, Patrick... this is *terrible*."

There were tears in her voice now, and unfortunately, I was going to have to be the voice of reason and pull her up and out of the hole she was in. That was my job. She was the anchor in our relationship, and I was the bunch of balloons that lifted her up.

"I know it is," I agreed with her. "We lived it and we know what we had to sacrifice to have our baby. And although I'm fucking livid at Axel—he knows better—Chastity's life is going to be very different than ours was."

"How so?" she whispered, still sniffling.

"Well, first of all, I assume she can still finish college and graduate." I hadn't done my calculations, but she only had a couple of months left and she'd said she was going to.

"Yeah, she can," Kaiti confirmed, her voice sounding soft and broken.

"Then that's one advantage. Yes, she won't be able to do chiropractic school yet, but it's possible she can at a later date."

Kaiti scoffed. "She'll never go back! You know that. Raising a baby by yourself is so hard... I don't know how she's going to do it."

I frowned. "What do you mean on her own?"

"You don't seriously think Axel and Chastity are going to last?" Kaiti spat. "They've known each other for all of a few months, Patrick."

I gripped the steering wheel tighter. I knew Axel, a lot better than Chasity or Kaiti, and he'd take this responsibility seriously. I believed it wholeheartedly, even if a part of me did want to punch him in his damn face. "Oh, I think you're underestimating their commitment to each other, sweetheart. They say they're in love."

She scoffed again, brushing me off.

I tried once more. "Axel has dated so many women over the years,

I've lost count, Kaiti. But he's never said that he loved any of them. And he has certainly never gotten any of them pregnant."

"So what?"

"So..." It was hard to explain to a woman how a man's brain worked. "He's serious about her, I know he is. A guy like Axel doesn't accidentally get a woman pregnant."

In fact, he'd told me in the past that he took his condoms home to dispose of if he had to. He was protective of his sperm, and that was understandable with his fortune. Gold diggers were always out there, women who didn't share Katherine's or Chastity's sense of morality and hard work.

"You think it was on purpose!" Kaiti gasped out.

Now I was rolling my eyes. "No. I don't think it was on *purpose*. I don't believe it was planned. But just like with you and me... when you're in love, you're not thinking about preventing future consequences. That's all I meant. That some part of him took the possibility into account and was okay with it, which means he'll support her and protect her."

"Financially maybe, but he's not going to be there changing diapers," she bit back.

No, he'll pay nannies to do that for him. "Sweetheart, look. I'm not worried about their relationship at the moment. We have no control over it, but we'll be there if Chastity needs us in the long run." Which she probably would. "I'm worried about you and our daughter. If you said all those things to her then I'm assuming she blew up?"

"She did," Kaiti confirmed. "And then she stormed out."

"And that's when she called me," I said, putting it all together.

"Oh, Patrick. What am I going to do?"

"You're going to get yourself a drink..." I began.

"I need a wine."

"Of water!" I finished. Giving up drinking entirely had been a little hard on Kaiti, but with the nausea she hadn't craved it as much. "I only care about your health at the moment. That's what we need to focus on. You and your pregnancy."

And that's when it hit me. I had a pregnant partner. *And* a pregnant daughter. I was going to be a grandfather. *Holy hell!*

"But Chastity needs us," she countered.

"Sweetheart, you just told her that she's making a massive mistake, which is going to drive her straight into Axel's arms. They're going to bond over this, the same way we got closer initially when your parents found out you were pregnant. Remember?"

Kaiti groaned in dismay. "Are you telling me that I just made all of this worse?"

"I'm not saying that at all, beautiful. I just want you to relax for the moment, to take a breather and let go. There's no easy solution to this one except time."

"Time? Really, Patrick? That's all you've got?" she snapped.

"Don't get shitty with me, please, Kaiti." I managed to get out through gritted teeth. "We're in this together, remember? You're pregnant, and our daughter is pregnant too. Both are huge things to deal with, and I'm on your side. Don't forget that."

I heard her huff and puff for a bit, then sigh in exasperation. "I really need something to eat. I might walk to a diner for a sandwich or something."

"That's a great idea, sweetheart. I'll be there in just over an hour. Can you send me the details of where you've parked?"

"Yeah, no problem. I'll text you now."

We hung up and I drove all the way to Chastity's school to pick Kaiti up. When I got there, Kaiti was standing by her old silver sedan, her bag slung over her shoulder.

She looked so beautiful with her hair out and flowing around her shoulders in dark waves. But she also looked tired, and her eyes were rimmed with red.

"Hey, good looking," I called out through my open window. "Can I give you a lift home?" I said with a smile, trying to inject a sense of levity into the otherwise fraught moment.

She didn't answer but climbed into the car anyway.

I looked at her, unsure of which way to go with our discussion. Was she angry? Hurt? Mad? All of the above? So, I opted for the safest thing I could think of. "Did you end up getting something to eat?" I asked. "Or should we stop for some takeout on the way home?"

She crossed her arms over her chest, still huffy. "I got something to eat. I'm okay."

"Then let's get going," I said, and put my foot on the gas as I pulled out into traffic. "You want to talk about it some more?" I said, sure that she still had things to get off her chest.

She wiped at her face, and I assumed she was crying again. "Not really. There's not much to say is there?"

"Well, there is. But if you don't want to talk about it, that's fine too," I soothed.

"I don't," Kaiti said, glancing out the window.

So, we didn't. We drove home, and she went to bed. I took a shower and called my cousin, who said he'd drive back to the college tomorrow with me to retrieve Kaiti's car. It was a time-consuming task, but I would never have forgiven myself if Kaiti had been in an accident while trying to drive home, stressed, angry, tired, and battling GD. She should never have gone up by herself in the first place.

Around dinner time, Kaiti surfaced looking pale and drawn. "I still can't believe it," she said, staggering over to sit down on the couch.

"Which part?" I asked.

"All of it," Kaiti said, pulling her hair up into a messy bun on top of her head. "Mostly that Chastity is going to have a baby."

I sat down on the couch opposite her. "Yeah, that's already kicking my ass, I have to admit. I'm going to be a grandfather." I shook my head and grimaced. "It's crazy."

"What if we can't sort all this out?" Kaiti whispered, her gaze plaintive, her anger cooled.

I moved over onto the couch with her and pulled her into my arms. "We will. Once everything calms down, we'll reach out to talk to her. But for now, you just have to concentrate on yourself, okay? Eat as often as you can, drink lots of water and sleep. All the things the doctor said to do."

She nodded and relaxed against me, her head on my shoulder. "I love you, Patrick. I'm so glad we found our way to each other again."

I chuckled softly and wrapped my arms around her more tightly. "I love you too, crazy one." I sensed Kaiti smile.

We had found each other again, that was all that mattered. It was a miracle on top of miracle. There would be fights, and problems, tempers and issues. But we were going to walk through the fire together this time, come hell or highwater.

I wasn't letting her go. Not now. *Not ever again.*

~

Read on for the final chapter in the Axel and Chastity saga: Second Chance Baby.
Available:
https://books2read.com/secondchancebaby